Anybody Shining

Also by Frances O'Roark Dowell

Anybody Shining

❧ ❧ ❧

by
Frances
O'Roark Dowell

Atheneum Books for Young Readers
NEW YORK LONDON TORONTO SYDNEY NEW DELHI

atheneum

ATHENEUM BOOKS FOR YOUNG READERS
An imprint of Simon & Schuster Children's Publishing Division
1230 Avenue of the Americas, New York, New York 10020

ATHENEUM BOOKS FOR YOUNG READERS
is a registered trademark of Simon & Schuster, Inc.
Atheneum logo is a trademark of Simon & Schuster, Inc.
For information about special discounts for bulk
purchases, please contact Simon & Schuster Special Sales at
1-866-506-1949 or business@simonandschuster.com.
The Simon & Schuster Speakers Bureau can bring authors to
your live event. For more information or to book an event,
contact the Simon & Schuster Speakers Bureau at 1-866-248-3049
or visit our website at www.simonspeakers.com.
The text for this book is set in Federlyn NF and Palatino LT.
Manufactured in the United States of America
0714 FFG
First Edition
2 4 6 8 10 9 7 5 3 1
Library of Congress Cataloging-in-Publication Data
Dowell, Frances O'Roark.
Anybody shining / Frances O'Roark Dowell. — First edition.
p.   cm
Summary: In a series of letters to her cousin, twelve-year-old Arie Mae relates
her life in a mountain valley of North Carolina in the 1920s.
ISBN 978-1-4424-3292-5 (hc)
ISBN 978-1-4424-3294-9 (eBook)
[1. Mountain life—North Carolina—Fiction. 2. North Carolina—History—
20th century—Fiction. 3. Letters—Fiction.] I. Title.
PZ7.D75455An 2014
[Fic]—dc23
2013032730

To Joy Salyers and Deborah Miller, my own true friends at the N. C. Folk Life Institute

Dear Cousin Caroline,
This morning I told Mama how I might have to run away and marry a bear if I don't find someone to call my own true friend. These mountains are near to spilling over with children, and none of them is worth two cents. They are all too old or too young or just plain disappointing.

It's the least fair thing in the world. James has got Will Maycomb down the road who is full of fun and mischief, and Lucille's friend Ivadee is a year younger but seems just the same as Lucille, wanting to play House and

School Teacher all the day long. Baby John is too young for friends, but when the time comes I am sure he will have a gracious plenty and I will still be sitting here on this porch by myself with so many things to say and not a one to say them to.

If you are a twelve-year-old girl looking for a friend in these parts, you are in a sad and sorry way.

The trouble about saying such things to Mama is that she'll make you regret it. "You have a nice cousin in Raleigh your age you could be friends with," Mama said. "It is a sin and a shame that you two don't know one another."

Daddy was sitting at the table working out a knot in Old Dan's harness. He looked up at Mama and said, "The reason they don't know each other, Idy, is because your sister don't want nothing to do with us, and she don't want her children to have nothing to do with our children. That's the sad but true truth."

Well, that set Mama to crying and moaning and groaning about how she was an orphan girl, her mama and daddy being dead and her only sister gone off the mountain to Raleigh to be a rich doctor's wife.

I could see that I was not helping matters by standing there, so I went out to the porch, where I do my best thinking. I sat on the steps and wondered how was I supposed to make friends with someone who I never even laid eyes on. That seemed fairly unlikely to me, especially if that person's mama was against the idea from the get-go.

Could that be true, Cousin Caroline? Does your mama really not want us to know one another? I've never heard of someone not wanting to know me. I surely want to know you.

I believe this is a matter that needs to be cleared up.

Here is how I come up with the idea to write my cousin Caroline a letter. I was out feeding

3

the chickens a few mornings later, happy to be outside, since Mama was in the kitchen, her face still full of gloom. I knowed that until we got Mama cheered back up again, life would be miserable for all of us. She'd forget to put sugar in her pound cakes and make us take baths twice a day. Why, she'd probably serve us bowls of water for Sunday dinner instead of chicken stew.

I felt so strongly that if I could just meet my cousin, we would become the best of friends, and that would make Mama happy. Maybe the thing to do was steal away on Old Dan and ride to Raleigh. The problem with that plan was Old Dan was not a good riding horse. He had ideas of his own about where to go and how fast to get there. Another problem was that I weren't quite clear on how to get to Raleigh, which would slow down my trip considerably.

Then I thought about how maybe I could hop the train that went down the mountain to Morganton, and then catch another train to

Raleigh. Then, when I got to Raleigh, I could buy a map and find my way to Cousin Caroline's house. But what if she weren't home? And what if I got caught riding the rails like a tramp? Didn't a person go to jail for that? Did they put twelve-year-old girls in jail? I reckoned they might, and then Mama would cry even more, and everybody would be more miserable than before.

And then it come to me. Why, making friends with my cousin was the easiest thing in the world! I stomped up the front steps to the house and found Mama in the kitchen.

"I am going to write Cousin Caroline a letter!" I told her. "Just give me a piece of paper and consider it done."

That cheered Mama up tolerably well.

Pencil and paper in hand, I walked out to the porch, sat down on the top step, and commenced to writing. After my introductory remarks, I added some things I thought Cousin Caroline ought to know about me straightaways. I thought it best to mention that I have light-red hair that some call straw-berry, but no freckles, and there are some that say I am cursed because of it. I don't believe in such a thing as curses. Dreama Brown's granny told us a tale of conjure ladies who live on the far eastern shores and wear gold hoops in their ears and put spells on folks. That sounds interesting to me, but I don't believe in it.

After I wrote about curses, I wondered if that was the right way to fill up a letter. What did children down in Raleigh talk about and think about of a day? How did they fill the hours? Did they have chores that kept them busy all morning, the way that me and James and Lucille did? Might could be that if your daddy was a doctor, you didn't have to do a thing in your life, just lean back on your fancy bed and eat candies that your butler handed you one by one.

What did I have to say of interest to a girl with a butler and probably a maid who but-toned the back of her dress every morning?

Well, I told myself, Lucille buttons my top back button for me, so that's almost like having a maid. I laughed to think of what a sad and sorry maid Lucille would make, bossing everyone about and saying, "You'uns pick up your own mess, I'm off to play tea party with Ivadee!"

Lucille would not think twice about sending a letter to our cousin, no matter how many butlers and maids they might have down there in Raleigh. That thought give me courage, and suddenly I had so many things to say, I didn't rightly know where to start.

My pencil raced down the paper as the words tumbled out. I wrote about the time Will Maycomb brought a live chicken in a flour sack for Sunday offering, and I wrote about the summer I was nine and went through a spell of sleep-walking, how I kept climbing out on the roof and Daddy ended up nailing my window shut, even though I never once fell off.

I wrote about how James got a fishhook

caught in his hand this past May and made me pull it out because the sight of his own blood causes him to faint straight to the ground. I wrote about our old dog, Bob, who run away when I was four and who I have never once forgotten.

I had about a hundred stories at the tips of my fingers, and I decided to write down every last one and let Cousin Caroline pick out her favorites. I sat there on the steps until supper, telling one tale after another, sure that once she read my letter, my cousin would certainly want to be friends with a girl such as myself.

I hope you will write me back, Cousin Caroline, and tell me such things as the color of your hair and when your birthday is and whether or not you like to read as much as James does. I don't care for reading myself, as I get squirrelly sitting all alone. But I like it when Mama reads to us of an evening from the books of Charles Dickens and Sir Walter

Scott, which a missionary lady give to her when she was but a girl over on Cub Creek Mountain, and your mama was also a girl sitting by her side.

Signed,
Your Cousin,
Arie Mae Sparks

Dear Cousin Caroline,

It has been a week since I sent my last letter. Now I am writing to wonder if you have received it. Was it too fancy and now you're shy about writing a letter back? Miss Sary says I am a good writer and have a head full of interesting notions, though there are folks in these parts who believe my ideas strange and far from sound.

That is what happened with Luranie Simms, who was a girl I thought I might be friends with once upon a time. By the end of our first meeting, I fear she thought me awful odd. She lives over to Bakersville, and one day last May my daddy was fishing in the Toe River and come across her daddy, and they got to talking. They found they had daughters of near about the same age and decided we should meet.

So on the following Saturday, after chores, Mr. Simms brung his Luranie over to the home place to visit. I had spent the week in a state of pure excitement and decided for the special occasion to write and perform a play for my guest. It was the story of the haints in our barn, and I called it <u>The Headless Haints and All Their Little Headless Haint Children</u>. I believed Luranie Simms would surely feel welcomed by having a girl such as myself write a play for her enjoyment and would want to be my friend and sit and talk and talk.

Sad to say, this is not how things turned out.

I wished I had some pictures to send to Cousin Caroline, so she could see in her mind everything I was telling her about, such as the Toe River and the plain-faced Luranie Simms. I think pictures make a story better, but since I didn't have a Brownie box camera like Doc Weems nor the talent to draw more than sticks and circles, I would have to draw my pictures with words.

The very minute Daddy told me that Luranie Simms was coming, I knowed we had to make a grand occasion out of it, and a grand thought come to me. I could put on a play! Wouldn't that just make Luranie Simms so happy, and wouldn't she see how good it would be to be friends with one such as me? Besides, I had the perfect story to tell. At last having a barn filled to the rafters with haints was going to come in handy.

I'd not seen the ghosts myself, but Daddy was all the time telling stories about them. He'd come in of an evening and say, "Well, if I didn't see Sam and Joe in Old Dan's stall smoking their pipes this afternoon! I was about to put up a fuss about the foolishness of smoking in a barn full of hay, but then them two old fellers just plain disappeared and took their pipes with 'em."

When I sat down to write my play, I started to tell about Sam and Joe, but I realized something pretty quick. For haints, Sam and Joe weren't all that interesting. Mostly, according to Daddy, they smoked their pipes in the barn or slapped Old Dan's flanks and spooked him. There weren't much of a story to that. But what if our barn was haunted by other spooky things? The more I thought about it, the more I convinced myself it must be true.

I went to find James, who was getting ready to go fish the creek. "What is the scariest kind of haint you can think of? So scary you'd run a mile in the other direction if you saw one."

"I think if I walked into the barn and saw old Sam and Joe, only they didn't have heads? Why, I'd probably fall over dead right there."

Now, James is a strong and sturdy boy who ain't scared of much other than the sight of his own blood, so I reckoned headless haints must be the scariest things going. But even better to my mind than a headless Sam and Joe was a headless Sam and Josephine and

13

some headless little babies. Oh, I liked that idea just fine!

To give credit, Lucille come up with the idea for costumes. I had planned on me by myself telling the story of Sam and Josephine and all their headless young'uns, acting out all the parts myself. When I told this to Lucille, she said, "Only problem is, you got a head."

We was on our way back from the schoolhouse, and I was trying to shake all the new learning out of my mind so I could get back to the business of writing my play. "Why is that a problem?" I asked.

"It seems to me your play would be a lot scarier if somebody without a head was part of the goings-on. 'Cause otherwise, it's just you telling a scary story and doing different voices. But if a headless person wandered out behind you while you was telling the story . . . well, that could have an effect on your audience, don't you think?"

"There's only one problem I can think of."

"What's that?"

"Everybody I know has a head. And I can't rightly imagine them agreeing to get their head chopped off for my play."

Lucille rolled her eyes, like she couldn't believe how foolish I was. "You just need the right costume, Arie Mae. Like, say if James put on one of Daddy's shirts, only before he put it on, he buttoned all the buttons and strung the neck closed. Then he could pull it on and the collar would sit on the top of his head, like he was Headless Sam."

I could just picture it. "And you could do the same with one of Mama's dresses. Only, how would you be able to move around without being able to see?"

"I could use a dress she put in the play-pretend box, and I could cut tiny holes where my eyes will be. And then I can hold James's hand while we're walking around behind you so he won't trip."

Well, didn't it work out exactly the way Lucille featured it? And weren't it the scariest thing in the world when we practiced my play with James and Lucille walking around without their heads?

It seemed like a hundred years between the time I woke up Saturday morning and the time Luranie Simms come walking up to the house. She was a drab-looking sort of girl, pale with skimpy brown hair, but her face warmed up with her smile, and I just knowed we was going to be the best of friends!

"I'll show you my room I share with Lucille and Baby John," I told her, "and then we can have a bite of something to eat, and then I'll do my play for you."

"You're going to do a play?" Luranie asked, sounding confused. "Don't you need all sorts of folks to do a play?"

"Oh, just you wait! You'll be surprised like you ain't never been surprised before!"

It's a funny thing to put on a play. Even if you have practiced it a hundred times, you will still fill up with butterflies before the show begins. Me and James had strung a sheet across the front porch to make it look like what we thought a real, live theater would look like, and we placed a chair facing the stage for Luranie to sit in.

"Ladies and gentlemen," I announced, coming out from behind the curtain, even though it were just Luranie in the audience. "Welcome to our show, *The Headless Haints and All Their Little Headless Haint Children!*"

Luranie got a pale look about her, and she scooched her chair back, like she wished to be as far away from the stage as possible.

"This is the true story of the headless haints that live up yonder in our barn," I continued, and I thought I saw a green aspect come to Luranie's pale face. "They are named Sam and Josephine, and they have a right fine passel of headless haint babies."

That's when Lucille come out from behind the curtain, her head hid underneath the collar of Mama's old dress. In her arms she carried her most wore-out and least loved baby doll, whose head she had detached for this occasion. A moment later, a headless James followed her out and bellowed, "Hello, Josephine, I'm home from the fields!"

Right about then is when Luranie commenced to crying, and then she run down the porch steps to the yard. She made a right good number of funny noises before she leaned over and was sick across the tops of her shoes.

It turns out that Luranie Simms is very scared of haints and all manner of spooky things, such as poltergeists, boogers, and most of all, the Headless Horseman of Sleepy Hollow. So I guessed I could see how my play might have troubled her.

Cousin Caroline, at first I felt as sorry as could be that I'd picked the wrong theme for my play. But while I was helping Luranie clean the sick off her shoes, it come to me that I couldn't have true friendship with a girl who turned green over a headless haint. I am as refined as any other girl you might meet, but I'm not a scaredy cat, nor can I abide one. I hope that you ain't scared by ghosts, poltergeists, haints, boogers, or made-up things that don't have heads. If you're scared of true living things that don't have heads, well, we are alike in that way.

Mama says she's worried she don't have the right address for you in Raleigh, but Daddy said that your daddy's people is high stock and fancy, and all my letters sent to Raleigh will reach them sooner or later.

If you're thinking my daddy don't like your daddy nor your daddy's people, you're right, but that don't mean you and I can't be the best of friends.

Signed,
Your Cousin Who Hopes You Will Write Back Soon,
Arie Mae Sparks

3

Dear Cousin Caroline,

I am still awaiting your fine letter. I think
you must be on a trip, as it's summer and
some folks like to travel during the pleasant
warm weather. I have never took a trip except
for the time we went to see Daddy's brother
Roland over in Buncombe County, who had
such pretty red horses. We have but the one
horse, Old Dan, and he ain't in the least way
pretty nor is he nice.

Today one of the songcatcher ladies, Miss
Pittman, come to visit. When she was talking
to Mama, I thought, I best remember

everything she says and does so I can tell it to my Dear Cousin Caroline in a letter. I have found that since I started writing letters to you I've been paying close attention to all the doings and comings and goings of a day. It's like saving secrets to share with a friend late in the evening, when the lights are dimmed but for a single lantern hanging on a neighbor's porch across the holler.

Do you have songcatcher ladies in Raleigh? If you don't, well, they are folks who come to your home place and write down the songs you and your family has been singing all through the years. Not only that, they have a machine the likes of which you ain't never seen. You sing into a big horn and the sound of your voice gets captured on a wax disc. Mama has done this two times now, and the first time we heard that wax disc played back to us, the sound of Mama's voice coming through the machine, why, I thought all of us was going to topple over from the shock.

* * *

21

Of the two songcatcher ladies, Miss Pittman is the friendliest. She don't look friendly, but that's because she wears her hair too tight on her head. It's pulled back like Samson himself took aholt of it and yanked. Lucille says it gives her a headache to look at Miss Pittman's hair. She is afeared that one of these days Miss Pittman's eyes are going to pop straight out of her eyeball pockets, her hair is pulled back so tight.

So Miss Pittman has a severe look about her, and she's hickory-switch thin, but when she opens her mouth and commences to speak, you see that she is actually quite jolly and full of fun. She also eats a bodacious amount, but no one can say where it goes, because she is all lean and no fat.

"Idy, you and I have got to talk," she said first thing upon taking her seat on the chair Mama had pulled out for her. It's the chair in least need of repair and saved special for company. "I know you think I'm nothing but a bother and a meddlesome pest, but we do so need your help at the settlement school. We have a group of visitors coming on Friday all the way from Baltimore, Maryland, and they would benefit so much from your singing."

Now, the settlement school was the school Miss Pittman and her colleague Miss Keller started last year. When they come to our mountains, they hadn't intended to stay much longer than a few months, but then they seen how poor some folks up here was, and thought a new school was just what we needed.

A settlement school ain't a regular sort of school. We already had us a regular sort of school up to the church, taught by Miss Sary, where children learned the usual run of things, reading, writing, sums, and such. No, folks of all ages go to the songcatchers' settlement school to learn practical things, such as how to make baskets and chairs to sell off the mountain so we won't be so poor, and how to practice good habits of health and hygiene.

The songcatchers is also interested in teaching girls how to bake beaten biscuits and light bread, and how to make hemmed tablecloths.

So there are lessons in cooking and sewing, too. Miss Pittman and Miss Keller have so many ways to improve our lot in life!

Daddy thought our lot in life was just fine, but he didn't turn his back on the settlement school until they come out against the Saturday night barn dances that he and Mr. Larry Peacock hold at Truman Taylor's place. Daddy and Mr. Peacock play radio music instead of the traditional mountain songs that the song-catchers thought they should stick to. That right there did the trick for Daddy, and we Sparks had to stay away from the settlement school from then on.

This was a disappointment to all us children, and I could see the disappointment written across Mama's face now as she answered Miss Pittman. "Oh no, ma'am," Mama said, taking her own seat across the table and picking up her piecework. She kept her eyes on her needle, but I could see from the way she was biting on her lip that she was near to bursting to sing at that school. "You know Zeke can't tolerate nothing

24

about that school. He likes you good enough, but not your school. He wouldn't never let me sing."

Miss Pittman twisted her hands in the folds of her skirt like she wished to be wringing my daddy's neck. "I just don't understand it, Idy. One of the purposes of the school is to preserve the music and the customs of these mountains. How could Mr. Sparks possibly have anything against that?"

Mama poked her needle in and out between two pieces of calico, one gray and the other one brown. She opened her mouth to speak, shut it again, and then finally said, "You like some of our ways, but not others. You like it if'n we sing you an old tune, but turn your nose up at a fiddle or a banjo."

"But the banjo isn't native to the mountains," Miss Pittman explained in a patient tone. "It's a corrupting influence."

"I don't rightly know about that, ma'am. I only know Zeke don't want none of us to have dealings with that school of yourn," Mama said, poking her needle hard through the calico fabric. "He says you'uns are outsiders and ain't got no business here."

Miss Pittman sighed, but she turned the talk to the peach tree blossoms that we are so enjoying right now and then told us children a story about when she was a girl in the state of Maine and a creature called a crab grabbed aholt of her finger and wriggled and wiggled and wouldn't let go.

I think it is purely a shame Mama can't sing at the songcatchers' settlement school. She has the highest, prettiest voice you ever heard. Some say it carries a lonesome sound, but I believe the lonesomeness makes it even prettier.

Miss Pittman stayed for lunch, which is her way. She ain't one to pass up the offer of food, which pleases folks considerably. There are some who come up to our mountains because they want to help us, but most won't never let you help them back. Miss Pittman ain't that way. If you give her a chicken, she won't say, *Oh, no, I could not take this, you are too poor to be giving such away.*

26

Miss Pittman will say, *Do you have any pota-toes I could cook up with that chicken?*

That's why folks like Miss Pittman so, even my daddy.

In fact, Daddy was mightily pleased when Miss Pittman and Miss Keller first come up to our mountains two years ago to write down our songs. He's a fiddle player and can learn a song off the radio faster than you can spit in your hand. When he heard the songcatchers had come, he took every spare moment to practice his songs so they would be just right for the listening.

On the day the songcatchers first come to visit, Miss Keller led the way up the path into our holler. She is stout where Miss Pittman is lean, though not so much in a round way as thick, and on that day she wore a black dress with a high collar that made me feel choky even though my own dress had no collar at all. I will say that Miss Keller has the prettiest brown eyes that spark at you when you say something that catches her interest. I don't like her as much I like Miss

27

Pittman, but I am always hoping for her esteem.

The two ladies was panting by the time they reached the porch, and had to catch their breath before speaking. We all just waited and a-waited, even Harlan Boyd, who by that time had come to live with us. Lucille was training Harlan to act right in company, pinching him when he spit or cussed or turned squirmy, so he was sitting straight as could be on the top step, still as a Sunday school boy.

"I am Louise Keller," the high-collared woman introduced herself once she was breathing normal again. "And this is my colleague, Betsy Pittman. We work for the Russell Sage Foundation. You might call us cultural explorers, which is another way of saying—"

"I reckon you're them songcatcher ladies we been hearing about," Daddy said, standing to welcome them. "My wife Idy knows many a song sung down from her granny and her granny's granny before her. As for me, I reckon I have a good fifty fiddle tunes I would be happy for you'uns to hear."

I thought I heard Miss Keller sniff at the mention of fiddle tunes, but how could that be? A fiddle sounds so sweet and will make you feel things so deep you will wonder why you don't bust open on the spot.

"We are most interested in the old ballads," Miss Keller explained to Daddy. "It can take a day, sometimes many days, to record a song correctly, so we will be taking up a good amount of your time. You'll have to come to the cabin where we keep our recording equipment, down at Katie's Fork. When would it be convenient to begin?"

Daddy looked at Mama. "Why don't you sing one of your songs, Idy? You could sing 'em 'Barbry Allen.'"

All us children clamored, "Yes, please sing 'Barbry Allen,' Mama!" even Harlan Boyd, who had taken to calling Mama "Mama" just as soon as Daddy had collected him from the old cabin on Cane Creek and brought him home to us.

Mama is shy about some things, but she ain't about others, so it come as no surprise when she threw back her head and commenced to singing.

All in the merry month of May
When the green buds they were swelling
William Green on his deathbed lay
All for the love of Barbry Allen

Miss Pittman covered her heart with her hands and closed her eyes, just taking in the sound of Mama's voice. Miss Keller whipped open a book, plucked a pen from a hiding spot behind her ear, and commenced to writing. I snuck over to her side to get a look inside that book and saw that it was just blank pages but for Miss Keller's twisty lettering. This was Miss Keller's songcatching book, and she carried it with her everywhere she went. At night, Miss Pittman would copy over in another book what Miss Keller had written down that day. That way, if one book got lost, they would have the other for safekeeping.

When Mama was done, we all just beamed

from our pride. Then we waited for the song-catcher ladies to ask Daddy to fetch his fiddle and play one of them tunes he'd been practicing so hard on. But they did no such thing, instead saying they would be back the following evening to hear more of Mama's songs.

They never did ask for Daddy to play his fiddle.

Cousin Caroline, does your mama sing the songs that got passed down from the old days? Maybe one day the songcatchers will knock on your door. Seems we get all manner of folks knocking on ours. Songcatchers, missionaries come to save our souls, all types of folks who want to help us one way or the other.

I wonder why there are so many folks who look at us and are unsatisfied by what they see?

I have asked Mama many a time to tell me about your mama, what she was like as a little girl, the games the two of them played growing up on Cub Creek all them years ago, and

31

why she decided to leave these mountains for good. But my questions bring a tear to Mama's eye, and Daddy is all the time telling me, "Hush now, don't ask no more questions about Anna, she is pert near dead and gone to us."

Well, as you might expect, that only makes Mama cry all the more.

When you write me back, I hope you will tell me all manner of things about my aunt Anna and whoever your daddy is. I know he is a doctor. Is he the sort that gives out red suckers to children? I have read about that sort of doctor in a book at school, and I thought it sounded right nice.

Well, Mama is calling me to go feed the chickens, so I will end here. Do you like chickens? I like them best for eating, second best for hearing them cluck in the yard first thing of a morning. It is a comfort, that sound.

Signed,
Your Cousin,
Arie Mae Sparks

Dear Cousin Caroline,

I fear you are ill. Get your mama to boil you up some comfrey tea. Comfrey tea will cure what ails you. I will be happy to receive your letter when you are feeling your old self again.

You'll be excited to hear them folks from Baltimore, Maryland, have arrived. Last night, me and James went over to Pastor Campbell's place to look at Miss Sary's book of maps called an atlas. We wanted to find out the exact spot where Maryland sits. Miss Sary, you will be interested to know, is Pastor Campbell's third bride. The first Mrs. Pastor

Campbell drowned in the New River five days after her wedding day. Ain't that the saddest story you have ever heard? The second Mrs. Pastor Campbell passed after taking ill with the influenza four years ago.

The newest one, Miss Sary, is about as new as they come. She ain't but twenty-five years old. Pastor Campbell went off the mountain to find her, and we was so happy he brought back such a young thing. It turns out she is filled with learning, too, which is why she has such books as an atlas and The World Book Encyclopedia, 1922, the one they made just two years ago. Oh, that encyclopedia is filled with so many exciting things! Me and James like to go visit of an evening just to look at the pictures. Have you ever seen a picture of a boa constrictor snake? It will curl your toes.

Maryland, it turns out, is two states above North Carolina. Baltimore is a large city where fishing boats bring to port such items as blue crabs, rockfish, catfish, and perch.

"It is a lovely city," Miss Sary told us. "We must go there on our travels one day."

Me and James and Miss Sary have all sorts of adventures planned for when me and James grow up. Miss Sary and James especially want to journey to the land of Brazil, but that's where they have them boa constrictor snakes, so I'm arguing against it. Couldn't we go to Peru instead? I suggest, but James is dead set on going to a jungle and shooting him a gorilla.

"Do they talk English?" James asked of the Baltimore, Maryland, children, for which I kicked his shin under the table.

"Of course they talk English, you ignorant boy," I told him. "They're in America. What else would they talk?"

"They speak English," Miss Sary said, resting a calming hand on my shoulder. "But they sound different from folks up here."

"Like you do?" I asked. Miss Sary is from Person County, close to Virginia, and when she talks it's more like someone singing to a baby. She is the prettiest talker I know.

Miss Sary laughed. "No, not exactly. Their talk is—well, flatter than the way you or I talk. Not as . . . curly."

That set James to laughing. "Curly? We talk curly? Who ever heard of such a thing as curly talking?"

"Oh, I don't know what I mean," Miss Sary said, blushing a pretty pink. "You'll just have to meet them. There will be several children your age."

Well, you can guess how them words excited me! The Baltimore children will be staying for a whole month while their folks study on the songcatchers' school so that they might start their own school for the fishermen who live up their way.

I wondered if the Baltimore children would find the settlement school disappointing. It is more like a house than the type of redbrick school you will see in books. They built it out of boards and made it two stories tall, which is unusual for these parts. Old Uncle Cecil Buchannan give the songcatchers twenty acres upon which to build and said they could cut all the trees they needed. All he asked in return is that they would put on a play by William Shakespeare now and again, as he thought it would be good for us children to see such a thing. When the songcatchers asked him if he had read Mr. Shakespeare's plays for himself, he said no, but he had heard tell that if you knew them plays and the Bible, you would know everything there is to know about how folks do and think and feel.

Inside the schoolhouse there are tables and chairs, weaving looms and cooking pots and chopping blocks, but no desks. There are many windows along the walls, so the rooms have a light and airy feeling about them. It used to be that we could go visit of an afternoon. That was before Miss Keller spoke out against the barn dances. I would sit in the front parlor of the songcatchers' school and smell the fresh-cut wood smell and oh, how I wished it were a school where you raised your hand and said the date of the Declaration of Independence and recited poetry.

When you look outside the front window, you can see the farm where they are teaching young men how to be farmers who make money. The man who is teaching them is named Mr. Gutterson, and he's from Denmark, Scandinavia. The way he talks sounds like nobody you have ever heard.

If you look out the back window, you can see several little buildings, such as a wood-working shop where they make split-bottom chairs, which are chairs with seats made from split cane or reeds, and other pieces of furniture to sell off the mountain. There is also a building for making pots, and another one for making baskets out of reeds.

If you look over toward the edge of the woods past the woodworking shop, you will see several cabins for the folks who come to visit from off the mountain. Of course that is where James and I went to search for the children from Baltimore, Maryland, last night after we finished our evening chores. We didn't tell Mama nor Daddy where we was going, though it's true I might have hinted we were headed for Miss Sary's. But we didn't ever say for sure.

"Those children won't want to know us," James said as we made our way down the path to the school. "Do you remember them ones who come up last fall, right after the school got opened? Their noses were stuck so far up in the air, a righteous rainfall would have drowned them."

"Children from Baltimore, Maryland, are different," I insisted. "They ain't snooty in the least. If they were, Miss Sary wouldn't say it was a pleasant city worth traveling to."

"Well, don't get your hopes up is all I'm saying."

Of course, James could say such a thing. He already has a true friend in Will Maycomb and don't have to worry about collecting more.

When we got to the school, we heard singing. I guess because it's a school started by song-catchers, they are always singing one song or another. There's morning singing after break-fast, and then end-of-day singing after supper.

Some Friday nights Miss Keller sends around word that they're having what she calls a Folk Sing, and everyone meets in the barn. Will Maycomb says that at the last one Mr. Gutterson taught songs from his country of Denmark, and Miss Keller and Miss Pittman showed off a dance from there too.

Daddy snorted when he heard this. "I guess we ain't good enough for them anymore. They have done got tired of our mountain songs and dances."

"Miss Keller and Miss Pittman learned some of their ideas from schools in Denmark," Lucille explained to Daddy. "And at those schools they sing Denmark songs and dance Denmark dances."

"They ain't in Denmark now," Daddy pointed out. "We got plenty of good dances of our own right here."

Mostly we have got the stomping kind of dances here, and I wouldn't mind to see a new step or two. But this ain't something I would say to Daddy, as he's partial to our ways.

40

James and I waited at the edge of the clearing for the singing to end. We couldn't decide whether we should greet the children when they came out of the barn, or if we should just spy on them to see if they looked to be the sort of boys and girls you could be friendly with. I thought we should spy for a bit and then walk over very natural-like and introduce ourselves.

I almost changed my mind when the Baltimore children come out and begun streaming across the field to the cabins. They were eleven in number and most of them was little, a couple were medium, but there was a boy and a girl who I could tell even from far away was about the right age, twelve like me or eleven like James. I squinted good at the girl, and will say that even from across a field she had a bossy look about her.

Do you know that kind of girl, the one who has a mouth set in a firm line like she's about to tell you what to do and won't never stop telling you what to do? Mariella Treadway is

41

just that way. We've been knowing each other since she come to live with her granny at the age of eight, and from the first second we was put in the same room, she commenced to bossing me about. "We will play tea party now," she told me, "so you go collect acorn caps for the cups."

Well, what I did was head straight for home. I ain't a disagreeable person, but I do not like being bossed by girls my same age.

So the Baltimore, Maryland, girl in the field was not promising. She had brown curls done up in ringlets, which is a pretty style that Lucille is always trying, though her straight hair won't hold a curl to save its life. The Baltimore girl wore a yellow ribbon in her hair, and her dress was yellow as well and looked store-bought. I looked down at my own dress, which was the brown one cut down from Mama's old everyday dress, and knowed I was in no state to meet a girl in store-bought clothes.

Oh, but the boy who was walking next to

her! Cousin Caroline, have you ever seen anyone who shined? Well, this boy did. Even though he walked with a limp and was a little bit sideways, he was shining.

And I thought to myself, Anybody shining, well, they are the one to be my friend. I'll tell you, up to then I'd always hoped my one true friend would be a girl, one such as who could talk about pretty things and would read poetry aloud with me. But when I saw the shining boy across the field, I thought him and me would be friends, even with the way he limped and was lopsided.

Sometimes you just know these things.

Signed,
Your Cousin,
Arie Mae Sparks

Dear Cousin Caroline,

This is the fifth time I have written to you. I have to say I am starting to wonder about the manners of folks who live down to Raleigh. I have heard of big city ways, and now I have to ask myself if some of what I've heard ain't the truth.

But I don't like to judge.

Lucille says maybe you don't write because your handwriting is a sight and mine is so very nice. If that is the case, I will tell you the secret of my nice writing. I have practiced it over and over until I made it just as pretty as could be.

In truth, I'm left-handed, but Mama wouldn't let me stay that way. She believes left-handedness is of the devil and ain't to be tolerated.

When I learned writing, the pen was placed in my right hand and it was so hard for me I cried and cried over it. But Daddy said he would buy me a bag of molasses candy if I could make my writing nice. I'll do almost anything for molasses candy. Also, I didn't want to write with the devil's handwriting. It's bad enough having light-red hair and no freckles.

My red hair is what caught the eye of the Baltimore children just as soon as me and James stepped foot into the clearing. One of the little ones pointed at me and said, "Look! She has hair the same as Cousin Clara!"

The tall, bossy-looking girl shook her head fiercely. "Clara's hair is brown with a hint of red when the sun shines on it. This girl's hair is practically pink, and quite unbecoming."

James whistled underneath his breath. "You still think them Baltimore children's so nice?"

"Not that particular one, no." I put my hand on my cheek, which felt hot, like someone had slapped it. "But she don't speak for the whole crowd."

"Maybe she does," James said. "You gonna wait to find out?"

A whispered voice popped up from behind us. "You want me to kick her in the pants, Arie Mae? I'll do it, just don't tell Lucille."

I turned around to see Harlan Boyd hiding behind a bush. If I ain't never described Harlan Boyd to you, well, he's a mess. He's ten years old, scrawny as a half-starved cat, with muddy freckles splashed all over his skin and brown hair that sticks up in clumps no matter how much he spits in his hand and pats his head.

"That's all right, Harlan," I told him. "Some folks just ain't partial to red hair."

"Some folks ain't got the manners that God taught 'em," Harlan replied, coming out from his hiding place.

"God don't teach manners," James told him.

"You're getting your Sunday school learning mixed up with what Lucille's learning you."

"It's hard to keep it all straight, that's a fact," Harlan admitted, shoving his hands in his pockets and taking a good spit at the dirt. Then he yelled over to the Baltimore children, "Hey, there, ya rascals! Leave ol' Arie Mae alone! She can't help how she looks, now can she?"

The bossy girl scowled in our direction, but that shining boy, he bust out laughing. Then he did something that purely surprised me. He reached over and yanked the yellow ribbon straight out of that bossy girl's hair. And when she screeched at him, he just shrugged and said, "Serves you right, Ruth."

Well, Cousin Caroline, I just had to go introduce myself to him right then and there. I tugged at James's arm, and the two of us walked right up to them Baltimore children. I stuck my hand out to the shining boy and said, "My name is Arie Mae Sparks, and I am pleased to meet you."

The shining boy didn't seem to know what

47

to do with my hand. In fact, he froze up the minute we walked over. The girl named Ruth tapped him on the shoulder and hissed, "Manners, Tom Wells!"

I dropped my hand straightaway. "It don't matter none. Not everybody cares for a hand-shake."

"Tom's just being timid," the bossy girl explained. "My brother is shy around strangers."

"No need to be shy around us," I told the boy, whose cheeks were burning bright red. "We're just regular children."

He'd been looking at his feet, but now Tom raised his head a bit and a smile snuck onto his face. "That must be nice."

"It pretty much is," I agreed.

"So," he said, and you could tell he was struggling to come up with something to say. "Well, I guess I was wondering, is—is it always so cold here in July?"

James stepped forward. "Son, sometimes it gets so cold, it snows the first day of August."

"No, it don't!" yelled Harlan, who had stood

back from the crowd, but now run over to join us. "That James will tell you a tall one, he sure will. It don't get cold enough to snow until nearly November, and then again some years it don't snow until come Christmastime."

Tom stumbled back a few steps, like he was afraid Harlan might plow him over. But he steadied himself and give Harlan a nod. "Right now, back where I live, it's hot enough that steam comes off the road after it rains," he told us. "If it's late in the day, it looks like ghosts."

"We ain't got no road here," Harlan admitted. "But we got us lots of ghosts!"

Tom's eyes turned bright. "Real ghosts?"

"Real as you're alive," I told him, cutting in before Harlan could tell all our best ghost stories. "We got a headless one living yonder in our barn."

The bossy girl named Ruth snorted. "Ghosts? In your barn? I guess no one has informed you that there are no such things as ghosts."

"You don't believe it? Just come up and look," I told her. "You'll believe it soon enough."

"Best ghosts are in the caves," James said. He leaned toward Tom in that confiding way he has that draws folks to him so. "Folks get lost in the caves, never to be seen again except as spooks and spirits. Why, almost any night, you can go over to Ghost Cave and see Wendell McBean right there at the mouth, asking you what's on the stove for dinner. Folks'll tell him, but he don't listen. Most spooks are stubborn that way."

Bossy Ruth shook her head. "Mother said we'd hear all sorts of stuff and superstition from people up here, and she was right. Tom, you're not to listen to one syllable of this nonsense."

Even though that Ruth was as bossy and rude as could be, I found that I admired the way she talked. It was like she was reading directly from a book. But one look at James and Tom, and I could see they didn't share in my admiration. I could also see that James was drawing Tom to him, and that if I didn't act quick, Tom would be his friend and not mine!

"Tom, I will be pleased to take you to the cave James is telling you about," I said, hoping to sound as refined as Ruth, but much more polite. "If you would like to meet me here in this very clearing tomorrow evening at this very time, why, I will show you the way."

Tom smiled at me. "I'd like that."

Ruth shot him a harsh look. "Mother will *not* approve," she warned him. Then she turned to the little ones. "It's time for you to be off to bed. Mazie, help me take these children to their cabins."

A girl of Lucille's age, which is to say ten, took the hand of the smallest child and turned toward the cabins. Ruth fussed at the others and soon was leading them in a line like a mother duck back across the clearing.

"We best be getting back too," James declared. "Daddy will set out looking for us if we ain't home before full dark."

"That's when the mountain lions will jump you," Harlan added. "If you're in the woods and hear a woman screaming, why, it ain't no woman at all. It's a mountain lion, and it will eat you tip to toe."

The light was draining out of the sky, but even so I could see Tom's face go ghosty pale. "Don't fret," I told him. "You'll be plenty safe here from all cats and wild things. Mountain lions don't prowl in the hollers. And if'n you do see one, just run away as fast as you can."

Tom looked shaky. "I can't run very fast. In fact, I can hardly run at all."

"Don't matter none," Harlan said, trying his best to sound reassuring. "Them cats are faster than us anyhow. You see one, you're licked from the get-go."

Tom did not look cheered by the news, but he give us a wave and said, "You better go before it's completely dark. I'll see you tomorrow, on this spot."

"This very one," I agreed.

Oh, and didn't we do just as we said, and didn't Harlan give us such a scare! But not one more word about it until I hold your letter in my hand and read the very words of your pen. I am sad to take such drastic measures, Cousin Caroline, but I feel you have been silent for far too long.

Signed,
Your Awaiting Cousin,
Arie Mae Sparks

Dear Cousin Caroline,

I have waited eagerly to hear from you after my last letter. Mama asked just this morning if you had wrote, and I was sorry to tell her no, not one word, and I wondered why not. "Maybe I should stop writing her if she ain't interested," I said.

But Mama said that was not the way. She said to keep writing you, and one day you would write back. "You've got to stay the course once you've started down the path, Arie Mae," she told me. "It is far too soon to give up. I once made the mistake of giving up

54

on someone too soon, and I have lived to regret it."

I asked Mama what she meant by that, but she just shook her head and handed me a pencil.

So I am not giving up on you, Cousin Caroline. I believe you will write me back, and I'm going to keep writing you until you do. But I am not going to tell you about how Harlan Boyd almost got murdered in the Ghost Cave BY A GHOST on Tuesday evening last until I hear from you, just as I said would be the case.

However, it is now Friday morning and my hand's itching to write something. Miss Sary says she has never met one such as me who is so eager to put words down on paper. I told her it's because writing things down straightens out my thinking and is almost as good as having a friend to tell all my secrets to.

So I will tell you the story of Harlan Boyd and his mama who left him to live all by hisself up in their cabin on Cane Creek.

Harlan's mama is named Earlene Boyd, and she's the same age as Miss Sary, which means she weren't but a young girl when she got married to Willis Boyd and had herself a baby. Everybody said it was a blessing she got married young, as she had hair the shiny black of a crow's wing and was known to be over-full of life, which is to say she was as wild as a rabbit in the fields.

But why you would marry yourself some-one as worthless as Willis Boyd is still a topic of conversation in these parts, even though no one has seen the man since the day Miss Earlene told him she was going to have a baby. Willis Boyd did not want a baby and made himself as scarce as scarce can be the minute he found out he was going to get him-self one.

It is a sad but true fact that Harlan has never once laid eyes on his daddy.

So Miss Earlene and Harlan lived by them-selves in a falling-down cabin on Cane Creek.

It got to be a habit with some folks to leave a little of what they had extra on the cabin's front steps. You could knock and knock all you wanted, but Miss Earlene would never answer, even if she was standing right there on the other side of the door, even if the person knocking was her own best friend, Wanda Coffey, which often it was.

For a long time, no one ever did see Harlan, and some said that there weren't a child at all up in that cabin with Earlene. They said she'd made a boat out of bark and twigs and sailed her baby down the creek for some rich family to find, the way Moses's mama did way back in Bible times. Others had more sinister plots in mind. They believed Earlene had murdered Harlan and buried his small bones deep beneath the cabin's floorboards. It was said if you stood outside the cabin under a full moon, you could hear his pitiful cries.

Well, all them stories was laid to rest on the morning that Harlan showed up at Miss Sary's school in the back room of the church, his knees and elbows scrubbed red, one shirttail tucked into his britches, the other one flopping out, the wore-out brown brogans on his feet a good two sizes too big. "My mama says it's time for me to get some learning," he announced. "She says eight years old is too old to be so ignorant."

All the children looked at one another, not knowing for sure who this boy was, but wondering all the same. Could it be?

"Welcome to our school!" Miss Sary greeted him brightly, taking him by the arm and leading him to her desk, which was really just a small table with her books and papers on it. "Let me write your name down, and then we'll find you a seat."

The boy went red to the tip of his ears. "My name is Harlan Boyd," he declared in an overloud voice. "And my mama says to tell you that I ain't stupid, just ignorant."

"My guess is that you're neither," Miss Sary assured him in that nice way of hers. "Why don't you stay inside during dinner, and I'll have you read to me?"

Harlan nodded and took a seat next to Lester Jones at the boys' table. I know I weren't the only one to notice that he didn't have a dinner pail with him, but when I peeked in the window at dinnertime, there he was sitting next to Miss Sary at her desk, chewing on a butter sandwich made with two pieces of light bread. Lucille, standing next to me on tiptoes, said, "Why, where'd he get that?"

"Miss Sary give it to him, I reckon."

Lucille shook her head. "Imagine not fixing dinner for a growing boy!" she said in that way of hers that makes her sound like a Sunday school teacher. "His mama ought to know better than send a boy down the mountain without something to put in his stomach."

And wouldn't you know, the next day Lucille wrapped Harlan Boyd two ham biscuits in wax paper and brung them to school. "A boy such as yourself needs some meat," she told him, shoving the biscuits in his hand. "You go and tell your mama I said so."

"I—I—I'll tell her," Harlan stammered, and

then he spent the rest of the morning eyeing them biscuits like a boy who had never seen such a wonder.

The next day Lucille wrapped up two more biscuits, just in case Harlan's mama forgot to pack his dinner again, and sure enough he showed up to Miss Sary's empty-handed. Lucille tsk-tsked and tut-tutted, and from that moment on Harlan Boyd was her project.

I don't think he minded too much, except when Lucille talked about visiting his cabin up on Cane Creek. "Someone's got to tell your mama to feed you better!" she declared. "I'm fixing to go up the mountain and tell her myself."

"She feeds me real good in the morning," Harlan insisted. "Eggs, sausages, biscuits and gravy, bacon and ham, why, it's all about to topple off my plate, they's so much food. That's why I don't bring no dinner. Ain't hungry again till supper after such a big breakfast."

Me and Lucille both doubted that story. We

were not the only ones distracted by his stomach's grumbles all morning while Miss Sary sat listening to us read from *The Beacon Primer*.

It was getting on into November, the sky gray and stretched thin, when Lucille took it into her mind to go ahead and do what she'd been threatening to do all fall. "Arie Mae, you come with me," she said late one Saturday afternoon, "in case they's any bears out there that need shooing away."

It's true that I'm not afeared of bears, so I agreed to come along.

So we trudged up the mountain, following the creek, until far up in a little clearing we saw the run-down cabin that belonged to Harlan Boyd and his mother Earlene. A sad little curlicue of smoke come out of the chimney, but we couldn't see or hear anybody moving about.

Lucille, who is afeared of bears but not much else, knocked firmly on the cabin door. Mind you, she was but eight years old at the time, come to give Miss Earlene a piece of her mind. It got me to giggling the more I thought about it. Who on earth ever heard of an eight-year-old bossing around a grown woman? Nobody, probably, until Lucille Sparks come into this land.

"Miss Earlene, I am here to talk to you about your boy Harlan!" Lucille called through the door. "He says you feed him breakfast, but I don't believe this to be the case. He is starving most every morning, Miss Earlene! His stomach growls like a lion! A boy needs to eat, Miss Earlene!"

Dead silence. I imagined Miss Earlene and Harlan standing on the other side of the door, shushing each other so that Lucille wouldn't hear them and would give up and go away.

If that's what they thought was going to happen, they surely did not know who they was dealing with.

"Miss Earlene! Open up!" Lucille shouted, and then she stopped shouting and commenced to throwing her little body at the door. "I'm busting in," she told me. "I have had enough of this nonsense!"

Well, I shook my head at her foolishness, but I climbed on the porch and threw my weight against the door too. No need for Lucille to break her shoulder.

After a few shoves, the door groaned open and we went reeling into the cabin. There, in a rocking chair by the fireplace, sat Harlan, still as midnight. The walls around him were gray and bare, the only spot of color in the room the red squares of the quilt laid across his lap.

"Where's you mama?" Lucille asked once she got herself steadied. "I come to talk to her."

"She's gone," Harlan replied matter-of-factly. "Been gone for about two months now."

"Where'd she go off to?" I asked, downright flabbergasted that somebody's mama could just up and leave that way.

Harlan shrugged. "Don't know. I woke up one morning and she weren't here. Thought maybe she'd be back soon, maybe with my daddy, but she never did come back."

"So who told you to go to school?"

Harlan shrugged again. "I told myself."

Sometimes when Harlan is getting on my last nerve, I think about what it must be like to sit by your ownself for two months, waiting for your mama to come home. Me, by the end of two months, I think I'd just have laid down and died. But not Harlan Boyd. He decided it was time to get on with his life, and that's just what he did.

You can't help but admire a boy like that. Even when he's just snuck under the table and tied your shoelaces to the table leg. You might clobber him, but you stay filled with admiration all the same.

Ever since Harlan has come to live with us, he can hardly sit still. He hops out of bed of a morning and is on the move from this spot to the next all the day long. Sometimes I wonder if I just imagined him sitting still as a stone in that rocking chair up in the cabin. After studying on the matter, I have come to believe Harlan knowed we was on our way to fetch him that day. I think he wanted us to see that he was a boy who could sit quiet as could be, if that was the sort of boy we needed him to be.

But that ain't the sort of boy we needed him to be at all.

Signed,
Your Cousin,
Arie Mae Sparks

Dear Cousin Caroline,

I keep thinking if I could tell you remarkable things, you would write me back. Who could resist a girl who writes stories of remarkable things? Like one about a boy who goes to scout out a haunted cave and comes running out, his face pale as the moon, crying that a ghost wrapped its ghosty fingers around his neck to strangle him? And sure enough, when the others stepped into the cave, moanings and groanings of a ghosty kind could be heard.

Harlan has admitted that it weren't really

a ghost trying to get aholt of him in the Ghost Cave, but only James pretending. So now I don't have that good story to tell you after all.

Turns out it was just James standing at the back of the cave, trying not to bust up laughing at the sound of his own terrible noises. I'm mad at my ownself for not figuring that out, but in the excitement of Harlan showing us the finger marks from where the ghost tried to strangle him—and there were marks, put there by James, it turns out—I failed to notice that James was not among us.

Ruth Wells looked suspicious when she seen them marks, but Tom? He got right up close and wondered out loud how was it that a ghost had bony fingers.

"There was no ghost," Ruth said with a sniff, before turning on her heel to head for home. "There's no such thing as ghosts."

"You don't know that for sure," Tom called to her back. "There's more to this world than meets the eye, Ruth Wells!"

I hope he won't be too mad when he finds out the truth. He don't strike me as the type who would mind a practical joke, even if he fell for it. Ruth, on the other hand, well, you can tell she's a person that would hate getting tricked. That's probably why she don't let herself believe in interesting things such as haints and boogers.

Me, I'm of the opinion you should keep your mind open to unlikely occurrences and events. I'd bet my bottom dollar that Tom Wells feels the same.

It was Miss Pittman who got the confession out of Harlan this morning. She had come up to the house to try yet again to get Mama to sing for them Baltimore folks. This time she picked a wily way to do it too.

"Maybe Mr. Sparks could accompany you on his fiddle," Miss Pittman suggested to Mama. They were sitting in the rocking chairs on the porch while Mama did her piecework and us children worked in the little garden out

68

front. It is a garden with such pretty flowers as lady slippers and fire pinks, and taking care of it is the only chore Lucille and I will fight to do. It seems everything we have got is made from faded-away colors like brown and gray and washed-out blue—our clothes and our quilts and the covers on the bed. But the flowers in our garden sing with pinks and reds and purples, and it's a pleasure to gaze upon them, even if it means mucking around in the dirt while you're plucking out weeds.

"I thought you'uns weren't interested in fiddles," Mama said. She looked up from her piecework. "I been wondering. Is it because you're religious?"

"I think it's mostly you Baptists who are against music and dancing," Miss Pittman replied.

"I thought everybody was Baptist," Lucille said from her perch on the steps. She had given up gardening to visit with Miss Pittman. "I didn't know there was anything else you could be."

Miss Pittman smiled. "Why, child, there are ever so many ways one can worship the Lord. Where I'm from, there are indeed Baptists, but there are also Methodists and Congregationalists, Catholics—"

"Now, do them Catholics believe in Jesus?" Mama interrupted. "I've heard some say that they don't. They got somebody they call a pope that they worship instead."

"My grandfather's people were Catholic," Miss Pittman replied, "and you can rest assured they believed in Jesus. The pope is just their religious leader, the way Pastor Campbell is the religious leader here for the Baptists, only on a much smaller scale."

I took this all in with some interest. Pastor Campbell is a Baptist preacher, and he is as nice as he can be, but he says that if you don't believe in Jesus, you'll go to hell, no two ways about it. But in Miss Sary's *World Book Encyclopedia*, there are pictures of children in India who follow a different way of thinking. They are called Hindu, and from how I read things they hardly give Jesus a second thought. I don't care to think of them burning in the fires of hell, and for my money I don't believe Jesus would care to think of it either.

"So if you go to Catholic church, you don't mind folks dancing and playing the fiddle?"

"No, I don't believe that Catholics mind music and dance at all."

I glanced up at Mama and saw she had that thinking look in her eyes. I bet she was wondering if she turned Catholic, maybe Daddy's barn dances wouldn't be a sin. Daddy was a Baptist, but he had fairly freewheeling notions of what made something a sinful activity, and dancing fell low on that list.

To my way of thinking, a barn dance is the best thing in the world. How they got started here is that last spring Daddy and Larry Peacock put their money together and bought a radio out of the Sears and Roebuck catalog, and then on Saturday nights they took it to Truman Taylor's barn and tuned it to the National Barn Dance on WLS radio out of Chicago, Illinois.

71

Most folks look forward to Daddy and Mr. Peacock's barn dances all week. You'll be in the middle of some boring old chore like beating out the rugs on the porch rail and all the sudden you remember that Saturday's a-coming. Your toe will start tapping its ownself when you think about all the good radio music you'll hear in Truman Taylor's barn. At the barn dances, folks jig and cut up and have themselves a good time. When the radio show is over, Daddy and Mr. Peacock get out their fiddles and play, and folks dance some more. The very thought of the good times ahead will pull you all the way through the week.

There are them who are against the barn dances. Pastor Campbell has made his stand clear on dancing, which is that it will lead to sin. Most Baptists other than Daddy believe this, but more than one will show up to a barn dance, because they been playing music in their families longer than they been Baptist.

It surprised a lot of folks when Miss Keller and Miss Pittman come out against the barn dances. For them, it's mostly because of the radio. Miss Keller told Daddy that the songs on the radio lack the nobility of our mountain ballads. "They are tawdry and full of cheap sentiment," she said.

"But folks like to dance to 'em," Daddy said. "You against dancing?"

"No, I am not," Miss Keller informed him. "But I am against throwing out the good and bringing in the bad. You have a tremendous tradition of music in these mountains. You should work to preserve it, not dilute it with silly songs about lovers' quarrels."

"Them ballads you like so much, what are they about other than lovers' quarrels?" Daddy asked. "You just like 'em 'cause they're old. Ain't nothing special about old. The songs we listen to on the radio, they'll be old someday too, and folks will jump up and down about how precious they are."

Now Mama, she loves the old songs just like Miss Keller and Miss Pittman, and like Pastor Campbell, she believes dancing leads to sin.

The problem is, ain't nobody on this mountain loves to dance better than Mama.

Mama didn't turn Baptist until she was fifteen years old, when she went to a tent revival and the spirit of the Lord entered into her and wiped her soul clean. Before that, her family read the Bible on Sundays and wouldn't work on account of the Sabbath, but they were not churchgoing. They could dance and play music to their hearts' content. Mama says she wishes she had been Baptist from the minute she was born, because then she would never have gotten the love of dancing in her and she would not have to try so hard to get it out.

"How you get to be a Catholic?" she asked Miss Pittman out on the porch this morning. "They let any sort of folks do it?"

"Yes, but I believe the closest Catholic church in these parts is in Asheville," Miss Pittman informed her. "Perhaps you should try the Methodist Church over in Spruce Pine."

Mama sighed. You could tell she weren't going to give up being Baptist, even if the pope

74

offered to take her out dancing every Saturday night.

"So do you think you would sing if Mr. Sparks played?" Miss Pittman asked again. "Perhaps the whole family could join you."

Mama's eyes sparked, and I knowed she was pondering whether or not she could convince Daddy to let her sing at the school. Mama loves to sing better than she loves to dance even, and singing for a crowd of folks is her idea of standing in high cotton.

Just then Harlan walked up from the barn, where he'd been helping James muck Old Dan's stall. "I'll sing. I'm the best singer you'uns probably ever heard."

Harlan sung about as well as a cat caught in a paper bag screeching to get out. Given this particular falsehood, I should have knowed he was capable of others.

"Tell Miss Pittman about the ghost that nearly strangled you," I urged. "She never believes me when I tell her about the ghosts in these parts."

The tips of Harlan's ears turned red. "Ah, she don't want to hear about no ghosts. Grown-up ladies ain't interested in them kind of things."

"On the contrary," Miss Pittman said, leaning toward Harlan. "I am riveted by such tales."

Well, by the time Harlan had tripped over his own tongue, mixing up the story so bad nobody who had actually been there would have recognized it, it was clear to Miss Pittman and everybody else that the whole thing had been a scandalous deception.

"You ain't right," I told Harlan. "You and James are the worst two boys I know."

"Ah, we ain't so bad," Harlan said with a grin. "We just like a little fun, is all."

I would have been madder at him than I was, but for the fact that I have made up some ghost stories myself once or twice. Between you and me, Cousin Caroline, I ain't actually ever seen old Sam and Joe who Daddy says lives in our barn. I don't think James has

either, but we both talk about it like we have. In fact, we may have convinced each other that them haints exist even though we know they probably don't.

At least I don't think they do.

Do you like ghost stories, Cousin Caroline? Because I know several that will send the shivers up and down your spine. Just the minute you write me back, I will tell them to you.

Signed,
Your Cousin,
Arie Mae Sparks

Dear Cousin Caroline,

You are not to breathe a word of what I am about to tell you! Today I snuck down to the settlement school so I could get better acquainted with them Baltimore, Maryland, children. I just had to go, is the thing. Why, I can barely sleep at night knowing them children is right down the mountain from where I lay, just waiting to be my friends.

It is easy enough to get to the settlement school from our home place. You follow the path that rambles alongside Cane Creek on its way to the river. It's been fairly trampled down ever since they built the post office next to the train station last year. Anybody looking for something to do will say, "I'm off to see what the news is," and head for the post office, where Miss Ellie Mize sorts letters and packages and collects the gossip. If you want to know who's sick, who's courting, or who got in a fight on Saturday night, why, it's to the P.O. you need to go.

Sometimes me and James go down to the train station to watch the three o'clock train come through. It don't stop unless there's a mailbag hanging on the post waiting to be picked up, but it always slows down. Me and James like to take a gander at the folks inside the train. We always wave, and some of them wave back while others act like they don't see us.

The settlement school ain't but a couple minutes farther down the road, and it don't take but maybe fifteen minutes to walk from here to there. The only problem is, Daddy don't want us to go.

Do you always do what your daddy says,

Cousin Caroline? Until the Baltimore, Maryland, children come to visit, I almost always did, partly because I try to be good when I can, and part because it don't pay to go against my daddy. He ain't mean, but he can be fierce as a bearcat when you vex him. James is the same way. Daddy is teaching James his habit of walking out of the room when his temper starts to rise. I have seen him do this on many occasions. To me, when Daddy leaves the room it is a sign to make yourself scarce as well.

Well, I don't like to go against my daddy, but I woke up this morning knowing that I must. It seemed clear to me that Tom Wells and I were meant to be friends, but how could we be such as that if I'm always here and he's always there? No, there weren't nothing to do but for me to go.

I done my morning chores as quick as I could, and then I found James over to the barn throwing slop into the pigpen. When I told him of my plan, he shook his head. "You know there'll be a price to pay if Daddy finds out you gone down there."

"But my chores are all done until the afternoon," I replied. "There ain't no law I have to stay put till then."

"But there is a law that says you're not to go to the songcatchers' school."

"All I'm asking is that you tell Mama and Daddy I gone to the post office to visit with Miss Ellie. And to make it the truth, I'll stop by and say hey to her on my way down the mountain."

James thought on that a second and said, "I won't tell 'em you gone to the school if'n I don't have to."

I knowed that was the best I'd get from James, who will joke and tell tales for fun, but when it comes to serious matters hates to be false. I didn't reckon they'd ask my whereabouts anyway. Mama and Daddy let us roam fairly free of a morning if we done our chores and weren't needed to take care of Baby John.

Oh, and didn't I feel so free as I headed

toward the creek! There was butterflies float-
ing across the sky and a breeze lifting up the
leaves, making a sweet hush sound over everything. A slew of birds chirped from their
branches, the bobwhite calling "Hoyee! Hoyee!"
and the mourning dove answering back with
its "Who-whoooo, whoooo."

I started thinking on all the fine things that
have come to our mountains in the last few
years. There's the settlement school and the
post office, Miss Sary, the barn dances, and
Doc Weems and his wife, Miss Olivia, who is a
nurse. They come up last year because Miss
Olivia has a lung sickness and the mountain
air is good for what ails her. She was at the
house on the night that Baby John was born
and helped Mama with the birthing.

And now them Baltimore children! They are
just one more good thing that has come to us,
I thought as I trotted down the path, and I felt
lucky to be Arie Mae Sparks who lived in
Stone Gap, North Carolina.

Here is another secret: the nearer I come to

the settlement school, the shakier my insides got. I've been knowing most folks around here since I first entered this world, and they are as familiar to me as the ten toes on my feet. But Ruth and Tom Wells and the others might as well have been kings and queens from Paris, France. What if they thought I weren't worth their time? Tom had been nice enough when we gone to the caves to see the ghost of ol' Wendell McBean, but we had been in a clutch of children, and it was too many of us to suss out his true opinion of me.

All I could do to ease my nerves was to say over and over, "You are a good girl, Arie Mae Sparks," which is what Mama says when I've pleased her. I singsonged them words all the way down to the post office.

"Well, hey there, Arie Mae!" Miss Ellie called when she saw me. She was leaning across the counter, not doing a thing but chomping on a piece of gum. "You got another letter to send to your cousin down in Raleigh?"

"Not today, but most likely I will tomorrow,"

I told her. "I just thought I'd wander in and give a holler, see how you was doing."

"Oh, my bones is tired and my head is aching something fierce. You ever heard of something called bursitis? I just read an article about it in the *Ladies' Home Journal*."

Sometimes I think I'd like to work in the post office, just so I could look at all the magazines that come through the way Miss Ellie does. Some folks complain about it, because she's always dripping her morning coffee on their copies of *The Progressive Farmer* and *The Saturday Evening Post* before they even get a chance to read them, but I don't drink coffee, so that wouldn't be a problem with me.

Miss Ellie went on for a while about the many things that ailed her, and then someone else come in and she shooed me away, like I'd been taking up her valuable time. So I headed on to the settlement school, telling myself what a good girl I was and remembering what Mama always says, that folks is folks, more alike than different.

The Baltimore children was all out in the big garden behind the main building when I got there. The garden is Miss Pittman's pride and joy, as they are able to grow most of the school's food in it. A fair number of the younger students live at the school and take their meals there. They come from Stone Gap, Bakersville, Cranberry, and Spruce Pine, and most of them are between fifteen to seventeen years old. The boys stay in a house called a dormitory to one side of the main building, and the girls stay in a dormitory to the other side of the main building.

Miss Pittman was standing in the middle of the garden when I got there, a hoe in hand, but when she saw me she waved and walked over. "Why, Arie Mae, I'm surprised to see you here. Is everything all right?"

"Why, yes, ma'am, I was just out walking and thought I'd come by and see how the children was doing. Pastor Campbell says that the practice of hospitality is the centerpiece of a Christian life."

Miss Pittman nodded her approval. "I fully

concur! As for the children, they are enjoying their morning in the fresh mountain air."

I couldn't help but believe Miss Pittman and I saw a different picture. Oh, a few of the little ones seemed to be having a fine time pulling up clumps of weeds and throwing them at each other, but the rest of them Baltimore children was leaning against their hoes and wiping the sweat from their brows. They looked purely miserable.

I searched the crowd for Tom and found him planted at the end of an okra row, peering at something he was holding. When he saw me, he held out his hand.

"This is an odd-looking creature," he called, pointing at the fuzzy bug crawling across his fingers. "I've never seen the likes of it."

"Why, that's a woolly worm," I informed him when I got close enough to see. "You can tell how bad the winter's going to be by looking at its stripes. See how some are black and some are brown? Well, if the brown stripes is wider, than the winter's going to be nice and mild. But if the black stripes is wider? Boy, it's going to snow something fierce and you won't see a thaw until April."

Tom watched as the woolly warm crawled from his hand to the edge of his sleeve. "I've heard a theory about acorns predicting winter weather. If the trees make more than the usual amount of acorns, it means the winter will be colder than usual. It's nature's way of providing for the squirrels. But my question is, how does nature know the winter's going to be bad?"

Now that brought up all sorts of topics for me. "Nature knows lots of things, and you can tell a lot of things by what nature does. Did you know if the sun keeps shining while it's raining, that means the rain won't last no more than half an hour? And if you see a crow flying real low, that means a big wind is commencing to blow."

Tom held up his hand, like he wanted me to stop. "Let me get my book out. I want to write all this down."

And then from his back pocket he pulled out

a book the size of a deck of cards. "I like to collect interesting information and stories," he
told me, brushing the woolly worm from his
sleeve onto the grass. "One day I'm going to be
an author or a newspaper reporter."

I had never met nobody before who wanted
to be an author or a newspaper reporter, and
right away I thought maybe that's what I'd
like to be too. "What kind of training do you
need for that sort of work?"

"If you want to be a writer, you write. At
least that's what my tutor, Mr. Sheard, says.
'Don't just want to be a writer, Tom, be a writer!'
He's always telling me that." Tom leaned
down and give his left knee a rub, like it
pained him. "Would you mind if we found
someplace to sit?"

"How about under that tree over yonder?" I
pointed to a pretty chestnut tree a little ways
away from the garden.

We sat down under the tree, and Tom took a
minute to get hisself comfortable. You could
tell his leg was a bother to him, and I wanted

to ask him what had happened to cause his limp, but I reckoned it wouldn't be polite. Instead I asked him if he'd written any stories yet or if he'd just been thinking about it so far.

"I've written a hundred at least," he declared. "I'm not much good at running or games, so I have a lot of time to write. I don't mind, though. I'd rather be writing stories than doing most anything else. Sometimes I make them up, and sometimes I visit my neighbors and ask them to tell me about interesting things that have happened to them. I practice my newspaper reporting skills that way. It's all about collecting the details, Mr. Sheard says."

"I wish there was more news around here to report," I told him. "You'uns coming up from Baltimore is the biggest news we've had all year. I guess it would be odd for you to write a story about yourself, though."

Tom give me a shy look. "If we worked together, well, I bet—I bet we could scare up some good stories. You could be my guide, and then Mother couldn't complain about me going off on my own. She's sure I'm going to be eaten by a mountain lion the minute I'm out of her sight."

I wanted to be a reporter alongside of Tom so bad the taste of it was in my mouth! Only I didn't know the first thing about collecting stories or how to go about finding interesting things to write about. Tom might be sorry he'd asked for my help.

But if you are looking for your own true friend, and somebody who might be your own true friend is sitting right next to you, you will make every effort to help them.

"I reckon I could come up with a hundred good story ideas if you give me time to think of them," I declared. "I just have to set my mind on it, is all."

Tom looked pleased. "Good. Now tell me more about this woolly worm, so I can get all the facts down in my book."

Well, Cousin Caroline, didn't we spend the rest of the morning trading stories back and forth beneath that tree? Oh, we talked over all manner of things, from the interesting ways of animals to our beliefs about the afterlife. I told Tom I reckoned heaven must look a lot like Stone Gap, North Carolina, and he reckoned he agreed.

When I got home for dinner, Mama give me a questioning look, but she never come out and asked me where I been. As for Daddy, he'd spent the whole morning in the upper field and never even knowed I was gone.

I am writing this letter in the last light of the day. In the morning I will walk it over to Miss Ellie at the post office, and maybe, just maybe, I will go visit the Baltimore children for a minute or two, hospitality being the centerpiece of a Christian life, as Pastor Campbell will tell you.

Signed,
Your Cousin,
Arie Mae Sparks

Dear Cousin Caroline,

Sometimes I wonder about writing these letters to you, just what good is coming of it? I know that it makes Mama happy for us to be friends, even if our friendship is only on my side, so that is one reason I keep writing. Also, I find that I like remembering the things I done of a day and what folks said and the thoughts that I thought. Sometimes I am surprised I have so much to write about. Turns out my life is fairly interesting, even if certain cousins of mine don't appear to agree.

Today I learned that there is another good

reason to write letters, and that is you never know who you will meet at the post office. Why, you might even run into your own true friend and have yourself an adventure.

Now Tom Wells was the last person in the world I expected to see as I come up the post office path this morning. Didn't he have something he needed to be learning, like how to make a chair or weave a basket? I didn't even know they let them Baltimore, Maryland, children off the school grounds by their own selves.

But there he was, sitting on the bench where me and James liked to sit to wait for the train. My heart quivered a bit at the thought Tom might be leaving, but then I noticed there weren't no packed bags by his feet, and I calmed down.

"Why ain't you at school?" I called as I run over to him. "You got skills to learn, son!"

"I spent two hours this morning learning how to weave a tablecloth on a loom. That's enough skills for one day." Tom waved a packet of letters at me. "Miss Pittman asked me if I'd mind posting her correspondence. I think she was trying to get rid of me."

"Why? Were you making trouble?"

"I think I was asking too many questions and they were getting in the way of her history lesson. I now know more about the history of looms and weaving than any other boy my age in the country."

I sat down next to him. "I think it would be right fun to make a tablecloth. Or anything like that. I never done it."

Tom looked at me all curious. "Doesn't everyone up here weave?"

"Not to my knowledge. I think my granny did, but now you can get cloth at the store. No need to make it yourself."

"I wonder if Miss Pittman knows that?"

"I think she's fairly against buying things at the store. She likes the old ways best."

Tom tapped his stack of letters against the bench so that they was all even with one another. "I don't have to be back at the school until noon. You want to go exploring?"

I glanced at Tom's leg, the one that don't work so good. Only the day before I'd been so excited by the thought of us having adventures and hunting for stories, but now I wondered if Tom was really up to tramping around the hills and hollers. "It's a lot of climbing to get anywhere around here," I said. "Lots of tree roots and rocks."

The color rose up in Tom's cheeks. "I can climb. I can do just about anything except run."

I nodded, figuring that Tom knew best about what he could and could not do. "That's fine then. Let's mail our letters and I'll show you the creek."

Now, Cane Creek is a well-traveled area, and mostly what there is to look at is birds and fishes and a snake or two swimming through the water. If you hear something crunching down the path, why, it's almost always someone on their way down to the post office or the settlement school. But I figured to Tom, who

95

growed up in a city, Cane Creek would be high adventure.

I had no idea how much adventure we was about to have.

Tom, as it turned out, was an admirer of rocks. "Look at that one," he said, pointing to a craggy piece of quartz crystal sticking out from the water. "I wonder how old it is? A thousand years? A hundred thousand?"

I'd not ever wondered about the age of rocks. They seemed like forever things to me, not items with their very own birthdays. "How can you tell?"

"There's a scientific method," Tom assured me. "But I don't know much about it. It has something to do with looking at the layers, I think."

I started examining the rocks along the creek bed. There was quartz crystal and limestone and lots of shiny mica. I reached down to pick up a piece of mica to show Tom how you could peel its layers off one by one, and when I looked back up, well, that's when I seen the bear.

It was actually a black bear cub, and it was

standing on the other side of the creek, looking over at us.

"Tom," I said, keeping my voice low. "If I was you, I wouldn't make any sudden moves. We're just going to back up real slow."

Tom, to his credit, did not startle or shout or even say a word. He just did exactly what I did, which was one slow step backwards, then another slow step backwards. Still talking soft and low, I said, "Now, you may not have noticed this, but there is a bear cub across the creek from us, and I can tell by the look in his eye he finds us a right interesting sight."

Tom stopped in his tracks. "I see him!" he said in an excited whisper. "Is he going to come after us?"

My experience with bears is fairly limited, but I have heard the stories from others, so I knowed what the possibilities was. "He ain't going to attack us, if that's what you mean, but if his mama is around, she just might. So the best thing is for us to move away real slow like we're doing."

But Tom had no interest in moving, it would appear. At least his feet had no interest. His hand was heading to his back pocket, where he kept that little book for writing things down.

"You can write about it later!" I hissed. "Right now ain't the time!"

Tom was already scribbling notes. "Right now is the only time! When am I ever going to find myself face-to-face with a bear again?"

"I'd say never, if his mama comes and eats you alive."

"Just give me one minute. Anyway, he's just standing there."

"It ain't him I'm worried about!"

I was in a pickle. I knowed the smartest thing to do was to get out of there as fast as we could without causing a commotion. And nobody was stopping me from doing just that. But I couldn't leave Tom, now could I? Who leaves their own true friend to get eat up by a bear?

"What's the difference between a black bear and a brown bear?" Tom asked. To his credit, he was still whispering, not that I thought whispering would keep us alive in the long run.

"There ain't no brown bears around here, so that's one difference. Can we go now?"

Tom held up a finger. "Just one more second. I want to describe how intelligent his eyes are."

I was starting to think that bear cub was far more intelligent than either me or Tom. He was King Solomon of the Bible compared to the two of us. I bet if he'd been in our position, he would have run off a long time ago.

He'd been standing there staring at us for a while, but now the cub turned his head toward the woods. I heard a rustling sound and knowed it was the sound of our doom. I grabbed Tom's arm.

"Mama bear's coming—let's get going!"

Finally Tom listened to sense, and together we backed up step by step until we were again on the path.

"Let's just get one look at the mother, Arie Mae," Tom pleaded. "I bet she's something to see, and we're safe up here, don't you think?"

This time I stood my ground. "I'll show you a picture of a mama bear in Miss Sary's encyclopedia, but if you don't move right now, then you will be the cause of my death."

I am pleased to report that the thought of my dying in the jaws of a bear made Tom feel bad enough to hightail it on up the path as fast as he could, which was faster than you might think, shooting a glance backwards every few seconds. Maybe I'm wrong, but I was pretty sure he was hoping that mama bear was hot on our trail.

That is just a little bit too adventuresome for my tastes.

We was huffing and puffing by the time we got back to the post office and plopped back down on the bench, holding our sides and breathing hard.

"We saw a bear, Arie Mae!" Tom exclaimed. "I can't wait to write Father about it!"

"Don't forget to mention the part where you almost got both of us killed."

Tom waved off my words like he was

swatting a pesky fly. "We were fine! We weren't in the least bit of danger."

I stared at him a long time. "You really are from Baltimore, Maryland, ain't you?"

"What do you mean?"

I shook my head. "I mean you sure ain't from around here."

That got Tom to laughing, and I started laughing too, and we just couldn't stop ourselves. We laughed so hard and so long that Miss Ellie come out from the post office to see what was wrong with us.

"You'uns go on home!" she yelled. "You're scaring off my customers!"

Tom got up to go then, but I said I thought I might sit a few more minutes. After Tom had gone, I let out a few more laughs, but the thought of my walk home sobered me up. What if that mama bear was on the path, looking for me?

Well, I thought, pushing myself up off the bench, at least Tom will be able to explain to Mama and Daddy what happened when all they find is my bones halfway between here and there.

And then I ran all the way home.

Now I suppose I might have come across that bear cub even if Tom hadn't been with me. Of course, I would have gotten away a lot quicker, having more sense when it comes to bears than Tom does.

But if Tom hadn't been there, why, it wouldn't have been an adventure, would it? It wouldn't be something I'll be telling folks about for the rest of my life. And I had that adventure all because I wrote you a letter, Cousin Caroline, and needed to mail it.

So I suppose I will write you another letter soon, even if you don't rightly deserve it.

Not that I am judging, because I don't judge.

Signed,
Your Cousin,
Arie Mae Sparks

Dear Cousin Caroline,

Last night I got to thinking about why you ain't written me back yet, and I have come up with a right good theory. You fear that your mama will be against it. Maybe she has said to you, "Caroline, under no circumstances are you to write a letter to that Arie Mae Sparks up there in Stone Gap, North Carolina! I don't care how many times she has written to you. If you don't answer her, maybe she will leave us alone!"

Well, you can tell that mama of yourn that I will keep writing these letters for the rest of

my life if that is what it takes to show you that
we are kin and should be the best of friends.

Besides, if I stopped writing you, how
would you know what me and Tom got ourselves up to?

Three days ago I walked over to the settlement
school to be neighborly, and who did I run into
first thing but Ruth Wells? And didn't I just
wish I'd worn me some shoes and maybe a
dress that didn't have a spray of spots on it
from the time Mama made me chop off a
chicken's head because she was too busy with
Baby John? I am here to tell you that a chicken's
neck will spurt blood something fierce the
second its head is removed, and it's better to
wear old rags to get the job done and not your
second-best dress.

Ruth come up to me with her fine manners
and said, "Arie Mae, I would like to meet
Pastor Campbell's wife, Sarah. Mother tells me
she comes from Virginia and was educated at
Hollins College. And now here she is, hidden

away in this primitive place. I think she must be fascinating!"

Primitive? I have never thought of Stone Gap as being primitive, but maybe you can't truly know the place you live in. Or maybe I don't rightly know what primitive means. I can report that the post office has electric lights, which seems fairly advanced to me.

But that was neither here nor there. "If you'uns come up the mountain after dinner tomorrow, why, we'd be happy to make your acquaintance with Miss Sary. She's about the nicest person I know."

Ruth smiled at me like I was a little child and said, "Why, thank you, Arie Mae. I knew I could count on you."

The more I thought about it when I got back home, the more I didn't want to take Ruth to meet Miss Sary. I was afeared she would turn her sniffy nose up at Miss Sary's humble home, even if she claimed she found her "fascinating."

But the minute Lucille heard that Ruth Wells was coming up to our house so we could take her to Pastor Campbell's, well, there was no turning back. Having heard me describe Ruth, Lucille could not wait to become her bosom friend. Lucille is drawn to ribbons and pretty gold lockets on thin gold chains, and bossy girls do not bother her in the least bit. It is girls like Lucille, the ones who are always trying to better themselves and other folks too, who are custom-made to be friends with girls like Ruth Wells.

I have to give Ruth one thing—she has pretty manners. She said, "How do you do, Mrs. Sparks," in a very friendly tone when James introduced her to Mama, and then she commented on Mama's piecework that was laying over the back of a chair. "Why, is that the Churn Dash pattern?" she wanted to know. "I hear that's very complicated."

"You know about piecework?" Mama asked, clearly amazed. "I didn't know folks off the mountain pieced."

Ruth smiled a gracious smile. "I don't actually make quilts myself, but Mother has an interest in domestic handicrafts. She is writing a book about quilts from the Civil War."

"Your mama's writing a book about quilts?" Mama looked over at one laid across the chair, then shook her head. "That's an everyday sort of thing to write about, ain't it?"

"That's why Mother finds them so interesting," Ruth explained. "They are everyday things, but they're also beautiful."

Mama continued to look doubtful. "I reckon."

As soon as Lucille got a taste of Ruth's refined ways, she run into the bedroom and changed into her Sunday best. I knowed she was wishing her Sunday best was a lot better than it was. When she pranced back to the kitchen, Mama took one look at her and said, "Uh-uh, Miss Lucille. You go right back in that room and change into what you had on. You'll ruin that dress tramping around in the woods."

Tears sprung up in Lucille's eyes, and I wondered how she was going to keep them from spilling over. But Ruth put her hand on Lucille's shoulder and said, "That's a lovely

107

dress, Lucille. It would certainly be a shame if it got torn or dirty."

Lucille sniffed a couple of times and looked shyly at Ruth. "Maybe we could stay here? I could show you my doll named Chandelier. Ain't that the prettiest name? I heard it in a book."

Ruth smiled, but she did not smirk, and that made me like her a little bit more than I'd been inclined to. "I would very much like to meet Chandelier. Why don't you change your dress, and then you could bring her with us to Mrs. Campbell's house? I do so want to meet Mrs. Campbell."

So off we went tramping through the woods to Miss Sary's, James and Harlan leading the way, followed by Ruth and Lucille dressed once again in her everyday clothes, holding Chandelier in her arms. I stayed to the back with Tom, who moved slower than the others on account of his leg.

"This is the greenest place I've ever seen," Tom said, looking all around him in wonder.

"Everywhere you look, it's trees and leaves and bushes and vines. I wish I knew the names of things so I could write them down in my book." He pointed to a bush with white flowers. "Like that!"

"That's mountain laurel," I told him, proud to have this knowledge, even though it's common to everyone around these parts. "It grows all over the place. It's nice, because the leaves stay green and shiny all year, and—"

Before I could finish, Tom quick put a finger to his lips, so I shut my mouth. He nodded his head in the direction of the left side of the path.

Well, maybe my eye caught a flash of light, like the wind had blown up the skirts of some low-hanging leaves, but I didn't see nothing other than that. "I missed it, whatever it was," I said.

"I could have sworn I saw somebody over there," Tom said, but he sounded doubtful about it. "A little girl in a white dress. She was—well, she was shining."

Oh, how I wished I could tell Tom I seen the

exact same thing he did. I would have lied if I thought it would make him be my friend, but I'm an awful poor liar, so he might not have believed me. "I might have saw something," I told him. "At least I *think* I might have saw something. Only I couldn't say what."

"It was probably just a bird," Tom said with a sigh. "Not exactly front-page news."

"If you saw something, then you saw something," I insisted, and then I had a right good thought. "Maybe it's Oza Odom you seen! They say she wanders up here. I ain't never run across her myself, but it might could have been her."

"Who is Oza Odom exactly?" Tom asked.

"Aunt Jennie Odom's little girl. Well, except that she's a ghost now. She died a long time ago. I don't rightly know from what."

Tom grinned, his spirits clearly lifted. "You didn't tell me there was a ghost up here!"

I shrugged, like I was used to seeing such things. "There's ghosts all over these parts. Dime a dozen."

We started up the path, both of us looking left and right for another glimpse of Oza, and when we reached Miss Sary's house, the others had just climbed the porch steps and were standing in front of the door.

"What took ya so long?" Harlan asked. "We was starting to think you got et up by a bear."

"We was admiring the scenery," I explained in my fanciest voice, trying to sound smart for Ruth. "There are so many lovely views in these parts."

Harlan give me a curious look. "You sound peculiar, Arie Mae. You ailing?"

Lucille leaned over and pinched Harlan hard on his arm. "Arie Mae has put on her company manners, and I expect you best do the same, Harlan Boyd."

Harlan spit off the side of the porch, like that was his answer. He seemed more interested in making an impression on the Baltimore children than staying in Lucille's good graces, something I reckoned he'd regret once them Baltimore children went home.

Miss Sary come to the door and welcomed us in. "You couldn't have arrived at a better time. I just made my special black walnut cookies."

Once we was all seated at the kitchen table, Lucille kept her eye on Ruth, copying her every move, including shaking out her napkin and spreading it across her lap like a blanket. You could tell she was trying her best to be dainty and ladylike. This did not stop her, however, from kicking Harlan under the table when he crammed three cookies in his mouth at once.

"What'd ya do that for, Lucille?" he wailed, spitting crumbs all over Miss Sary's pretty tablecloth. "You ain't supposed to kick when you're company!"

Lucille just shook her head. "You are like to be the death of me, Harlan Boyd."

That's when Ruth took charge of the conversation, asking about Miss Sary's people and her schooling and if she enjoyed mountain life even though she was an outsider.

"Oh, I don't feel like an outsider at all!" Miss Sary exclaimed at that last question. "This is the most beautiful place I've ever been, and everyone you meet is so welcoming and generous. People are always bringing us such wonderful things to eat. Pastor Campbell says we live among the salt of the earth, and I couldn't agree more."

"But don't you find it difficult to talk to those so different from yourself?" Ruth asked, taking a bite of her cookie. "What could you possibly have in common with the people here?"

Well. My mouth fell wide open at that. Who was Ruth Wells to decide that Miss Sary wasn't one of us?

Miss Sary looked thoughtful. "Well, I know at least two people who share my love of encyclopedias and world travel," she said, smiling at me and James. "I had to come to the mountains to find friends who had that in common with me."

Ruth seemed to consider this, but she didn't

say a word back, just took another cookie from the plate. You could tell she thought Miss Sary was merely being polite.

I decided to take this opportunity to seek out some news for our reporting project. "You ever see anything shiny out in the woods here, Miss Sary? 'Cause me and Tom, well, we saw something on our way up today."

Before Miss Sary had a chance to answer, Ruth turned to Tom and demanded, "What's this about?"

Tom looked like he'd rather not say, but Ruth kept glaring at him, so I reckon he felt like he didn't have a choice. "I thought I saw a girl in the woods, and Arie Mae's right—she was sort of shining. But then she disappeared." He glanced over at Miss Sary. "Arie Mae said maybe she was Oza Odom."

Miss Sary nodded. "Aunt Jennie's little girl who died of a fever. I expect that's who it was."

"I heard she just wanders around night and day looking for her mama," I said. "Is that the story you heard, too?"

"The very one," Miss Sary agreed.

Tom reached into his back pocket for his book. "What can you tell me about Mrs. Odom?"

"Aunt Jennie? Well, she lives over near Pilgrim's Gap," Miss Sary said, "about a mile and half's walk from here. She's close to a hundred years old and stays by herself. I visit her the first of every month, and she's always doing something interesting. Last time I was up there, she was writing down all her recipes—her receipts, she calls them. She said she'd heard tell of such a thing as a library, and she thought any library worth its salt would certainly want a collection of her recipes."

"Ghosts," Ruth said firmly, "are for weak-minded people."

Miss Sary just smiled at her and held out the plate of cookies. "Have another, won't you, Ruth?"

Me and Tom exchanged a look. We didn't even have to say what we was thinking. We was going to track down Aunt Jennie Odom and find out about her daughter, Oza. If there was truly a ghost living in these woods, why, surely that was news worth reporting.

After we finished eating cookies, Miss Sary got out her atlas, and we had a time pointing out all the countries we wanted to visit. Ruth said she wanted to go to Africa and see the tigers, and James said he thought tigers mostly lived in India, and they argued about that for a while until everybody felt wore out and fidgety and we went home.

Oh, but didn't I lay in bed that night with a grin plastered across my face? Me and Tom had us a story to report. We would track down that shiny girl, Oza Odom, and we would write up her tale just like real authors. Why, I could hardly get to sleep just thinking about it.

Tom and I have made a pact to go to Aunt Jennie Odom's on Friday, three days from now. In between now and then he is hoping the cut on his hand will heal. When I asked him how he got it, he said it was from making

116

a split-bottom chair. He was weaving reeds together real tight for the seat when one of the edges sliced his finger.

I never knowed anybody who made a split bottom chair before the songcatchers started their school, but Tom says they are a mountain crafts tradition. Sounds like an awful dangerous tradition to me. I think I'll get my chairs from the Sears catalog, if it's all the same.

Signed,
Your Cousin,
Arie Mae Sparks

Dear Cousin Caroline,

Mama and Daddy had the biggest quarrel this afternoon, and anybody could have told you how it was going to turn out. My daddy goes around acting like the boss of everything, but in the end Mama always manages to get her way.

We children weren't meant to overhear, of course. We'd been out picking peaches for to make peach butter and weren't expected home for some time yet.

It was on account of Lucille getting stung by a bee and having a fit that we come home

118

early. Now, most folks will cry a tear or two when they get stung, as it hurts so awful bad, but Lucille acted like she was breathing her last. Since folks have been known to die on account of a bee sting, me and James decided we best not take any chances, even though we knowed it was probably just Lucille making much ado over a tiny thing.

By the time we reached home, Lucille seemed to have recovered, though she kept a hand over her eyes so we would know that she was still suffering in her soul. James and I helped her up the porch steps, but just as James was about to pull open the door, Daddy's voice come out the window and froze us all in our places.

"Idy, I won't have you singing for them folks. They have come up here trying to change our ways to their liking, and I won't put up with it."

"They say they're trying to preserve our ways," Mama's voice come in reply. "That's why they want me to sing for them Baltimore people, so that they can truly know what mountain singing is."

"Oh, they're fine with our ways from a hundred years ago. It's our ways of today they don't like so much. It's like we're supposed to be froze in time. Don't ever turn on the radio, they say, don't ever read you a newspaper that someone brung over from Asheville. You might get corrupted."

"Miss Pittman said you could play your fiddle, Zeke. Wouldn't you like to play your fiddle for a crowd?"

"Not that crowd," Daddy said. "They don't know enough about fiddle-playing to appreciate it. Besides, I'm tired of playing them old songs."

"Yes, Zeke, but the songs you like so much are ones you learned off the radio. They ain't our songs."

"I make 'em mine by playing 'em," Daddy argued. "They're mine soon as they go in my ears and come out my fingers."

"But you play the old tunes real pretty, Zeke.

I bet folks at the songcatchers' school surely would like to hear that. And maybe you could make some kind of trade with Miss Keller and Miss Pittman. Maybe you could play some new tunes after you got done playing the old."

There was a stretch of silence after that, like Daddy was pondering. Me and James looked at each other. We was dying for Mama to sing, and it would make us proud to hear Daddy play in front of them Baltimore folks. Maybe if all went well, Daddy would let us go to the settlement school now and again after we got done with our chores.

"Idy, I will tell you what," Daddy said finally, and by this time, even old Lucille was up and leaning her ear against the door. "I will make a trade. You can sing at the songcatchers' school if them two ladies will come to a barn dance of a Saturday night."

"Consider it done, Zeke Sparks!" Mama exclaimed, sounding livelier than I have heard her sound in some time.

I don't know that the songcatcher ladies will

be as enthusiastic about this trade as Mama seems to think. I can't quite figure them out when it comes to things changing and things staying the same. At the settlement school, they teach folks new ways of cooking and farming and cleaning up a home and tending to the sick. So they favor some new ways of doing things, and don't mind changing us mountainfolk in those regards.

But I heard Miss Keller once say she wished the Sears and Roebuck catalog had never made its way to the mountains, because people were abandoning the homemade and traditional for store-bought.

I don't know why this bothers Miss Keller so. Daddy ordered Harlan Boyd a guitar from the Sears and Roebuck catalog Christmas of last year, and you should have seen Harlan's eyes shine when he come into the sitting room Christmas morn. He didn't care a lick who had made that guitar or where it had come from. And Lucille got a pretty Sunday dress made from yellow fabric that Mama never could have found at the dry goods store. All them things seem fine and good to me. But to Miss Keller and Miss Pittman they are signposts on the path to ruination.

There are many things about the song-catchers' way of thinking I don't quite understand. Tonight, after supper, James's friend Will Maycomb come for a visit, and he told us something that has troubled me considerably.

Will's sister Thelma is one of them who attends the settlement school during the day and then comes home at night, so the Maycombs know about as much as anybody as to what goes on down there. Miss Pittman is training Thelma to be a secretary, which is one who helps out in a business office typing letters. Many an afternoon Thelma works in Miss Pittman's office, helping her put papers in files and organizing her letters.

"Well, today, she was straightening out papers on Miss Pittman's desk when she come across a carbon copy of a letter that Miss Pittman wrote when she was starting the school," Will told me and James, the three of us sitting on the front porch steps. "Now, you'uns know Thelma and what a busybody she is, so of course she read it. Turns out, it was a letter asking someone off the mountain for money, and the whole thing was about how backwards folks are in these parts. Miss Pittman said she couldn't believe the condition folks lived in, that people lived in filth and ignorance. That was an exact quote from the letter—'filth and ignorance.'"

"Miss Pittman didn't write any such thing!" I cried. "Why, she's our friend!"

Will shrugged. "She might be your friend, but she sure don't think too highly of you."

James leaned forward. "Maybe Miss Pittman was making things sound worse than they were so she could get more money. If she told 'em that we was all doing fine and didn't need much help at all, they probably wouldn't send her a dime."

"Could be," Will said, not sounding worried about it one way or another. "But my mama's fixing to go down there and give her a piece of her mind. Told Thelma she weren't to go back in the morning, but Thelma says she's sewing on a dress she wants to finish before the next dance, so she's going back anyway."

I thought maybe I'd go down and give Miss Pittman a piece of my mind myself. But just the thought of standing in front of her and crying out, *How could you?* set my lower lip to trembling. There are the Lucilles of this world, who put their hands on their hips and fuss and fight, and then there are the Arie Maes, who just store things up inside and never say a word. I wish I was the other, but I am myself and not good for making a scene. So I just sat on that porch and looked at my feet and felt the shame settle deep inside.

Well, pretty soon I just had to go inside and lay across my bed. Did Miss Pittman really think us ignorant and backward? Maybe James was right, and she had to say such things to get the money to run her school.

Still, I hated to think of people off the mountain believing we live in filth, when that's the furthest thing in the world from the truth. Why, Mama won't hardly let us go out of the house if we've got a speck of dirt under our fingernails.

Is that why you never have written me back, Cousin Caroline? Do you think I'm backward? I hope it ain't so. I hope you can find it in your heart to reconsider.

Signed,
Your Cousin,
Arie Mae Sparks

Dear Cousin Caroline,

I have terrible news. We have been invited to a picnic.

Now, usually I will jump up and down at the news of any kind of gathering where there is food and games and maybe a song or two. It is not uncommon to have church suppers on summer Sundays, and we children have the best time! We play Anty Over, where you have two teams, one on one side of the house, and one on the other side. One person tosses a ball over the roof, then runs fast as a deer to the other side to see if the ball is caught. If not, he gets the ball back. If so, the catcher runs around to the thrower's side and tries to tag people with the ball. Another game we play is town ball, which Miss Sary says reminds her of baseball, only in town ball, you get runners out by throwing the ball directly at them. Miss Sary disapproves of that part of the game, but all she will say is, "Just don't throw that ball at me!"

So you would think that I would be happy to attend any picnic I was invited to. But this particular picnic invitation come from Miss Pittman, and I wish like anything I didn't have to go.

It was Ruth who brung the invitation. She come up yesterday morning with her little cousin named Mazie tagging along behind her. I was hoeing the garden to the side of the house when here come the two of them looking fresh and clean. Mazie is Lucille's age, and you can see she is training up to be just like Ruth when she gets older. She holds herself

128

straight and fine when she walks. They was both of them wearing blue dresses with white sailor collars, long white socks stretched up to their knees, and black patent leather shoes. Ruth was wearing a white ribbon in her hair, and I bet it was killing Mazie that she didn't have a ribbon herself.

"Good morning, Arie Mae!" Ruth called out when she saw me. Whenever Ruth says a word to me, her tone sounds halfway between making fun and nice. I can't quite figure her out. She's bossy, but she ain't quite as awful as some bossy girls I have knowed. Still, I don't ever feel at ease with her.

"Hey, Ruth!" I called back, brushing some dirt off the skirt of my dress and wishing like always when I saw Ruth that I had shoes on. "Lucille's gone with Mama to the dry goods store, but I reckon she'll be back soon enough."

"We can't stay but a moment," Ruth told me. "Mazie and I have slipped off from a sewing lesson, and we're expected back soon. But we were so excited, we just had to come tell you.

Miss Pittman and Mother have decided to have a picnic for the local children tomorrow, in the clearing by the creek behind the cabins. It's going to be such fun!"

My first feeling upon hearing this news was disappointment. Now Tom and I would have to put off our trip to find Aunt Jennie Odom! My next feeling was that I did not particularly care to spend time with Miss Pittman, even at a picnic. How would I even look her in the eye, knowing what she thought of us?

"Do we have to dress up for this picnic?" I asked Ruth, wishing I had a basketful of ribbons to put in my hair so I could impress Miss Pittman with how civilized I was, not filthy in the least.

"No one need dress up, especially as we'll be having games," Ruth told me, Mazie nodding solemnly behind her. "You don't want to get your best dress dirty, now do you? Besides, Mother was concerned that if we asked people to dress for the picnic, some of the boys might not come."

"She said most of you don't even have nice

clothes," Mazie added. "And it would embarrass you to show up all plain and degradated. So we are to wear our plainest dresses to make you feel more at home."

"Hush, Mazie!" Ruth hissed. "You'll make Arie Mae feel badly about the things she doesn't have."

"That's all right," I mumbled, feeling not even one inch tall. "I got nicer clothes than this. I just don't like to dress up to hoe."

"That's exactly right," Ruth said, nodding her approval. "Of course you wouldn't wear your Sunday best to work outside."

"I got at least five dresses," I lied. "Though one or two may be getting tight. I guess Mama will have to take me shopping over to Asheville soon enough."

Well, I have never been to Asheville nor worn a store-bought dress in my life, but you will say all sorts of lies when you're feeling not even one inch tall.

"The best dresses are the ones the dressmaker makes," Mazie informed me. "Mrs. Green on

Eager Street. Ready-made dresses seldom fit properly."

"That's enough, Mazie," Ruth said. "Not everyone can afford Mrs. Green."

"Mother says—"

"Enough." Ruth give Mazie an icy glare, and Mazie's mouth clamped shut.

"So, tomorrow then, Arie Mae," Ruth said, turning to me. "Tell Lucille and James and Harlan we very much look forward to seeing them at noon. Mother and Miss Pittman have all sorts of treats planned. Be prepared for an afternoon of delights!"

I watched them two walk down the hill toward the road, and then I went and sat on the porch steps to recover from their visit. I was still setting there worrying about that picnic when Mama and Lucille got home from the store, where they had gone to fetch coffee and sugar and some nails for Daddy. I knowed my only hope was that Daddy would say no to Miss Pittman's invitation. But for all that he did not care for the settlement school, Daddy thought it poor manners to turn down an offer of hospitality, and he might make us go.

"You finish up in that garden yet, Arie Mae?" Mama called when she saw me. "You got to get them weeds before they take over."

"I'm almost done, Mama," I replied. "But before I get back to it, I best tell you the news."

This picnic Miss Pittman has planned is going to be as hard on Mama as it is on me. I only have myself to worry about, but Mama must add James, Harlan, and Lucille to her list. It's important to Mama that her children make a good show in the world. We may not have pretty ribbons or handsome suits, but we're to have the nicest manners and the cleanest faces and the best-combed hair. When she gets us ready for church on Sunday morning, it's like an army general preparing troops for battle. Fetch me that scrubber brush! she yells. Harlan, you best wash behind your ears, they's a garden growing back there! Arie Mae, your braid's coming undone and you look like a wild thing!

"Oh, Lordy," Mama moaned when I told her of Miss Pittman's picnic. "She sure didn't give us much time to get ready. We'll wash clothes this afternoon and the children this evening. And we'll have to prepare some vittles for you'uns to take."

"Ruth didn't say we needed to bring anything," I told her. "I believe they're fixing all the food themselves."

"But you still carry something with you, Arie Mae!" Mama exclaimed. "You can't just walk into somebody's place empty-handed. I know I raised you better'n that!"

Then she got to worrying about what she should fix. It had to be something that didn't need to be hot to taste good, and it had to be able to travel down the mountain to the song-catchers' school. "I'd have to use the last of our dried apples to do it, but an apple stack cake would be a nice treat to send," Mama declared after pondering on it a few minutes. "I got a box saved you'uns could carry it in."

"Yes, Mama, make an apple stack cake!"

Lucille exclaimed. "Yours is the nicest one anybody's ever had."

And it's true, Mama's apple stack cake is well appreciated in these parts. She brings it to most every church supper, and folks clap their hands when they see it, it tastes so awfully good.

"Well, I will make it first thing tomorrow morning," Mama said. "So it will be as fresh as can be for your party. Now, come on, girls. We need to go see about the clothes for you to wear."

It was time to play my only card. "Daddy ain't gonna like this," I told Mama as she hurried across the porch to the door. "He don't want us to have nothing to do with that school."

"This is different, Arie Mae," Mama said. Her point was just as I feared. "This is an invitation to a party. It's hospitality, and we don't turn down hospitality when it's offered."

That is how we come to spend the rest of the day getting ready for Miss Pittman's picnic. When Daddy, James, and Harlan come in from the high field, they fussed at Mama for making such a poor showing for dinner, just heated-up soup beans, not even a pan of cornbread, though James brightened some at the news of the picnic. It was like he'd plain forgot that Miss Pittman thought we was filthy and ignorant.

"I hope they got races and swimming!" he exclaimed. "And strawberry ice cream, too."

"Strawberry ice cream?" Harlan asked, as if such a thing were beyond all belief. "Sign me up for that!"

Cousin Caroline, I am writing this letter late at night. I can't sleep for thinking on all the things that might happen tomorrow at Miss Pittman's picnic. What if there's special forks and spoons that we don't know the proper way to use? What if I spill all over myself and Tom pretends not to know me? What if in the middle of a polite conversation, Harlan starts to spitting and cussing, in spite of all the training Lucille has give him? I fear we will behave in such a way that Miss Pittman will think she's right to say that we are uncivilized, ignorant folks.

Maybe I will wake up tomorrow with pneumonia and will have to stay home. That is what I'm hoping for, leastways.

Signed,
Your Cousin,
Arie Mae Sparks

Dear Cousin Caroline,

There is such a good deal to tell you about all that happened today. Most of it I'd rather not think about ever again, but if I don't write it down, then I won't have no peace in my mind. There is a voice asking why write it to you, when you don't ever answer back, and I wonder that myself. Maybe now I'm just in the habit of it. Maybe I'm in the habit of believing that you read my letters and care what I got to say, even if you don't write back.

Maybe you got two broke hands. If so, I am

sorry to hear it, but that sure would explain things.

I'm writing this beneath the window of the room I share with Lucille and Baby John. Moonlight is streaming in and lighting everything up, so it's just as good as having a lamp by my side. I've been gazing at Baby John's face, which is as round and ruddy as an apple. For so long he was the prettiest baby you have ever seen, and he's still nice to look at, but he's coming on nine months and not so much a baby anymore. You can see in his face the little boy he is about to be.

Sometimes I think it would be nice to be Baby John's age again and have no worries. Today, walking down the mountain to Miss Pittman's picnic, carrying Mama's apple stack cake in a box tied up with string, I worried about being ignorant, and I worried about the dress I was wearing, my blue everyday, the one that shows the least wear and tear, but is still drab and dreary. With it I wore my brown lace-up oxford shoes and white socks.

James and Harlan went barefoot, but I couldn't bring myself to do that, even though my brown oxford shoes are too tight.

Lucille and I trailed James and Harlan to the cabins where the Baltimore folks was staying. The closer we got, the slower and slower my feet moved. You are a good girl, Arie Mae Sparks, I told myself over and over, but I did not feel good. I felt like nothing about me was good enough, not my dress, nor my shoes, nor the words I spoke or the thoughts that run through my mind.

I used to be so happy that the songcatchers had started their school here, even if I couldn't go. But now I wished they'd never come, so I would never have these bad sorts of feelings about myself and everyone I know.

We could hear the laughter of children as we got closer, and suddenly I thought to wonder what other children would be there. Will Maycomb and Ivadee Ledford, I supposed, along with all their brothers and sisters, and I wouldn't have been surprised to come across Addie and Billy Eckley nor Minnie, Carl, and Caroline Vinson. I thought of all the houses you will find along the road from the settlement school to the Hollifields' place on the highest perch of Pumpkin Patch Mountain and counted up a righteous number of young'uns. What would them Baltimore children make of us all gathered together? I shuddered to wonder.

Well, it was quite a sight when we rounded the corner of the visitors' cabins and headed in the direction of the creek. All the children I have named and plenty more was running wild as unbroken horses in the grass. The Baltimore children stood to one side and looked on as though they was watching a show. Every last one of them wore shoes, and their faces was shiny clean. The mountain children looked more used up and most had dirty feet.

As soon as she saw us, Ruth called out, "Arie Mae! Lucille! Come help us set the table!" She sounded as though she was doing us an honor by asking. I thought it odd that there was tables for a picnic, but it turned out to be just the one for setting out food and another for plates and punch. When it come time to eat, we would spread out blankets on the grass and sit with our plates in our laps.

We followed Ruth into a cabin where platters of food were laid out upon a table. "Miss Pittman and Mother thought sandwiches were appropriate, and I agree," Ruth told us, pointing at the food. "At first we considered beef and pickle sandwiches, but in the end decided that cream cheese and olive would hold together best."

Lucille and I nodded, though we are not much for sandwiches as Mama don't make light bread, which is the kind you can slice into thin pieces to put something between. Mostly we have biscuits and cornbread. Still, I have seen pictures of sandwiches in magazines, so the sight of them weren't shocking.

But olives and cream cheese? I glanced at Lucille and saw her lower lip a-trembling.

Lucille is one of them who is particular about what she eats and don't take to unfamiliar food easy. When we attend a church supper, she'll stick to whatever Mama has made, in spite of all the ladies who urge her to try just one bite of their famous dishes.

"I am sure you and your mama have made the right choice," I told Ruth, setting down Mama's apple stack cake on the far end of the table. "Cream cheese and olives sounds like a treat."

"You don't think the mountain children will find them too unfamiliar?" Ruth asked. Her tone made me suspicious. Maybe she hoped we would turn on our heels at the sight of such food and run back up the mountain, showing ourselves to be ignorant and plain.

The sandwiches was cut up into triangles and set upon pretty platters. There were also bowls of nuts and cucumber spears, and plates with sliced radishes and tomatoes and hard-boiled eggs. While there was plenty of everything, it seemed to me a meager spread, nothing there

143

to fill your belly. Still, I thought maybe this was how high-class folks ate, and I swore to myself that I would try a bite of everything.

A tall woman with a crisp, white apron tied around her waist walked into the room, looking brisk and full of good cheer. "Hello, girls!" she called when she saw us. "I'm Ruth's mother, Mrs. Wells. You must be Ruth's friends Arie Mae and Lucille. Now, which one is which?"

I could tell from the second I laid eyes on Mrs. Wells that she was who Ruth got her bossy side from. From the very manner in which she walked into the room, her head turning this way and that, making sure all was as it should be, it was clear she was in charge.

"I'm Arie Mae Sparks, ma'am," I said. "And this here is my little sister, Lucille."

"'This is my sister, Lucille,'" Mrs. Wells corrected me. "Say things directly, Arie Mae, and you'll be better understood. From looking at the two of you, it is clear that Lucille is younger than you are, and the use of 'here' in that

144

sentence was extraneous. Now, let's carry these platters outside and tell the children it's time for luncheon."

That's when I wanted to tell her that she'd fixed all the wrong sorts of food for the mountain children, who would have as soon chucked a radish slice through the cracks in the floor than eat it, but I suspected she would not have listened to me. Mrs. Wells did not strike me as the sort who listened to anybody but herself.

I followed Lucille over to the table and was about to pick up a plate of buttered bread, when Mrs. Wells said, "Arie Mae, may I speak with you for just a moment?"

"Yes, ma'am," I replied. Lucille give me a worried look and I give her a look that said, *Don't you never mind.*

"It's nice to finally meet you, dear," Mrs. Wells said after Ruth and Lucille left. She leaned over the table to neaten a row of radish slices on one platter, then straightened a line of carrots on another. "You and my Tom have become friends, I understand. I'm very happy that you children have accepted Tom with such open arms. Sometimes people find it hard to overlook his—his difficulties."

"What difficulties would those be, ma'am? Do you mean his leg?"

She nodded. "His leg, his limp, the fact that he can't run and play like other children. For a boy his age, it's quite a handicap."

"I don't mind none. None of us children do. Everybody's happy for Tom to be here."

"You don't mind *any*," Mrs. Wells corrected me. "You must learn to speak properly if you're to advance in this world, Arie Mae. Now, Tom tells me you two plan to hike through the woods tomorrow to a place called Pilgrim's Gap."

"That's right," I told her. "We aim to find Aunt Jennie Odom. Tom wants to collect some of her stories."

Mrs. Wells frowned. "Yes, well, I'm afraid such a journey will not be possible. You see, it's not only Tom's leg that bothers him. Tom had scarlet fever as a young child and it weakened his heart. Therefore I must ask that you not overtire him. He wants to do things that normal children do, but he simply cannot."

My knees got a little bit wobbly when she said that, and my fingers and toes went cold. I have knowed children with weak hearts, and they ain't often long for this world.

"Arie Mae, this is strictly confidential." Mrs. Wells leaned toward me and put a hand on my shoulder. "You mustn't tell Tom I've told you this. He doesn't know how damaged his heart is, because he's never been one to overdo and I haven't wanted to worry him. But since we've come to the school, I suspect he'd climb a mountain every day if he had the time. But he can't, and he mustn't. Do you understand what I'm saying, Arie Mae? You must keep him to quiet activities when the two of you play together."

"Yes, ma'am," I said. "I'll be careful not to wear him out."

"Good," Mrs. Wells said with a nod. "Now carry these things outside. I believe Miss Pittman

147

is about to lead the children in a game of Mother May I, and when that's over we shall eat."

Well, I carried that bread and butter tray outdoors with a heavy heart. I had never felt sad about Tom's leg, at least not too sad, because it seemed to me he made do right well on one good leg. But a weak heart was another story. A weak heart was not to be messed with. Now I'd have to come up with lies to tell Tom about why we could not go to Aunt Jennie Odom's or even trek up to see Miss Sary. I ain't as strict about the truth as James is, but to lie to Tom seemed to me a terrible thing.

When I got to the yard James had all the children, even the ones from Baltimore, tied up in a game of Green Man's Garden. Now, Green Man's Garden is a right good game if you have enough children to play, so I could see why James done it. What you do is divide into two sides. One side starts the game by calling over, "Where are you?" and the other group calls back, "In the green man's garden!" First group says, "What are you doing in the green man's garden?" and the second group might reply, "Eating the green man's grapes!"

To that the first group calls out, "The green man will get you!" And everybody starts running around then, the first group of children trying to catch the ones in the garden. If you get aholt of somebody, you throw them into the soup pot.

Now, what James had done was get the mountain children and the Baltimore children all mixed up, so it wasn't one group against the other. And everybody was laughing and a-running and having a jolly time. But Miss Pittman was standing to the side, next to Ruth, and I could tell from the way her lips was pressed together in a thin line that she did not like this game one bit! You could see she thought it was a low-down, mountain children's game and that Mother May I was the game we all should be playing.

Part of me had been itching to get into that game myself, but then I seen Miss Pittman's face and also I seen Tom sitting off to the side, wishing like anything he could play too, and it about broke my heart.

"James!" I cried out. "Put a stop to this right now! This is not the game Miss Pittman is wanting us to play!"

But James didn't listen, nor Harlan nor Will Maycomb. Them Baltimore children didn't listen either. Well, that got me angry as a wasp trapped in a jar. Did they think they didn't have to listen to me? So I run straight into the middle of the crowd and grabbed James by the arm. "You are a rude, ignorant boy! Quit this game and show some manners!"

James's face got still and white, which is how you know he's angry something fierce. "You let go of me, Arie Mae," he said in a quiet voice. "Or else I'll make you wish you had."

I dropped his arm, but I stood there glaring at him for a good, long minute. "You show some hospitality to Miss Pittman," I hissed at him finally. "This is her picnic, not yourn."

James shook out his shoulders like he was getting shed of me and walked away. "Game's over," he called to the crowd. "Miss Pittman wants us to play her game."

The children moaned and groaned, the Baltimore children loudest of all. Miss Pittman clapped her hands and smiled grandly. "Line up in two rows for Mother May I," she commanded. "And after that, luncheon!"

I looked over to where the table was loaded down with platters of olive sandwiches and sliced cucumbers. I'd not yet carried the apple stack cake from the kitchen, and now I couldn't bear the thought of them Baltimore children laughing at it, the way I was sure they would. And so I run back into the kitchen, and I shoved Mama's cake in the cold stove.

I hated to do it, but I hated worse the thought of them children turning up their noses at Mama's cake that she worked so hard to make.

The worst thing? Later, when James asked me where the cake had got to, I told him I didn't know, but I bet one of them Baltimore children chucked it out the window! That got him and Harlan riled up, and they left even before the ice cream was served, without saying a word of good-bye or thank you.

And even worse than the worst thing? James lied to Mama about it when we got home and said her cake had been everybody's favorite. I knowed he hated to lie, but he would have hated hurting Mama's feelings even more than lying.

I write this with such a heavy feeling inside of me. And on top of all the other things plaguing my mind is how I'm going to tell Tom tomorrow morning that we can't take our trip to Aunt Jennie Odom's. That's all he talked about at the picnic, me just a-nodding and a-smiling, even though I knowed we weren't ever going to go up to Pilgrim's Gap.

Oh, James ain't the only liar living in this house.

Signed,
Your Cousin,
Arie Mae Sparks

14

Dear Cousin Caroline,

By the time Tom got up to the home place this morning, I had worked up a terrible story to tell him. I had thought about saying I didn't feel well, but then he would have said that we could go tomorrow or the next day, and then I'd just have to act sicker and sicker until I was lying in bed pretending to be half-dead.

So I decided the only thing to do was tell him I had no interest anymore in Aunt Jennie Odom or ghosts or the stories Tom wrote in his little book the size of a deck of cards. It killed me to even think about saying that, but what else was I supposed to do?

Oh, it made me so mad that I finally had a true friend and he was living at death's door!

When Tom showed up, I was sitting on the front steps shelling crowder peas, the last of my morning chores. "I fear we have to call off our trip," I said as soon as I seen him, wanting to get it over with. "Mama and I had a long talk last night, and she don't want me believing in ghosts. It goes against the Bible."

Another lie. They was starting to pile up like the stacks of apples in Mama's cake, and my stomach hurt with each new one.

"Still, don't you think it would be interesting to meet Aunt Jennie Odom?" Tom asked, limping up to the porch. "Mrs. Campbell said she must be nearly a hundred."

I threw an empty seedpod into the yard. "Sounds dull as dirt to me. I bet her brain is addled."

"That's not how Mrs. Campbell made her out. She sounds fascinating."

"If collecting recipes sounds fascinating, then I guess so. But it don't to me. I think we should stay here and sit for a while, and then we can walk down to the post office to see Miss Ellie. She's always got a good story to tell. We could do some good reporting down there."

Tom give me a funny look, and then he just shook his head. "No, I plan on going to Pilgrim's Gap. If you don't want to go, then at least tell me the way."

I looked at my feet. "Don't rightly know."

"Fine then," Tom said, turning on his heel. "I'll find the way myself."

Well, Pilgrim's Gap is a good two miles from here, through rough woods. I threw down the bowl of peas I'd been holding in my lap and headed after Tom, who was moving fast for a boy with a bad leg. "You'll get eaten up by a bear," I called out. "Or a wasps' nest will fall out of a tree and land right on your head, and then where will you be? All stung to pieces is where!"

Tom kept on walking. "If you're not going with me, then at least stop yelling. I can't hear myself think."

Tom's back was turned to me, like he wanted nothing more to do with the likes of Arie Mae Sparks. Well, I just couldn't bear that for a second! Without even thinking, I yelled, "Your mama says you ain't supposed to!"

I swear I didn't mean to say that, it just come out. Tom whipped around.

"What has Mother told you? Some story about my heart, I'll wager. She tells everyone the same nonsense. Father says it's because she was so worried about me when I was a baby that she can't break the habit."

I ran to catch up with him. "So you know about your heart?"

"I know that Mother tells everyone it's weak and that I'm not to move a muscle, but my heart is fine. Even Dr. Hatcher says so! Maybe a bit weaker than other boys' hearts, but I can do whatever I want. It's this bad leg that holds me back, not my heart."

156

I looked at Tom's leg and wondered again how it got bad in the first place. I studied on Tom's face. Was he telling me the truth? There was a nervous edge to his tone, like he was testing out those words for the first time. But I had never knowed Tom Wells to be a liar, and I thought if you had yourself a true friend, you ought to believe him.

"So it won't kill you to walk to Pilgrim's Gap?"

"Not unless a bear eats me," Tom said with a grin.

And so I decided to go with him. I even decided to tell him the truth about my lies. "My mama didn't really say I couldn't believe in ghosts," I admitted as we entered the woods. "Fact is, she believes in ghosts more than anybody I know. She'll scare you to death with some of her stories."

"My father likes to tell ghost stories," Tom said. "He claims to have seen the ghost of his dead grandmother when he was a boy. She leaned over his bed in the middle of the night and said, 'Tell your mother not to worry.'"

"About what?"

Tom shrugged. "She didn't say."

I found that a satisfying reply. "That's what makes a story sound real, when there's some mystery in it," I said. "Stories in books have explanations for everything, but real-life stories don't so much."

Well, that's how it went the entire way up to Pilgrim's Gap, me and Tom talking about interesting things the way we do when we're together. He told me some more about his daddy, who is a lawyer and spending the summer in Baltimore working on a big case about property lines that Tom said made him want to fall asleep every time he heard about it. I told him the story about Harlan Boyd and another one about the time James and me got caught on the wrong side of Cane Creek when it flooded and had to spend the night with Mama's great-aunts, three ancient old ladies who don't never go to bed and smoke pipes all night long so that you can't hardly breathe to sleep.

Even if we'd never found Aunt Jennie Odom's cabin, I would have said it was a fine trip. But when we reached Pilgrim's Gap, we saw the chimney smoke swirling in the air and knowed we had found the place we was looking for.

"You'uns see Oza on the road?" Aunt Jennie asked us matter-of-fact when she opened the door, looking for all the world to me like a dried apple doll. She was more wrinkle than smooth, like the shell of a walnut, with a backbone bent like a question mark. "That's what brings strangers here, Oza stirring up trouble."

"Is Oza your—your daughter?" Tom stammered out, and Aunt Jennie nodded.

"She wanders the woods the livelong day, and ever' once in a while she asks folks to show her the way home," she told us. "Only, she knows the way already! That's why I get so wore out with her. You see her over to the pastor's place?"

Tom nodded, and Aunt Jennie give out a little "Hmmph!" before saying, "She does it to irritate that man, I swear. Baptist preacher don't want nothing to do with no spirits. The Bible's a-gin it. Well, you two children come on in and I'll feed you'uns. You ought to get something for your troubles."

Aunt Jennie's cabin was tiny, but it was cozy how I like, with everything in its place. There was a bed made up with a pretty coverlet tucked in neat, and a table with two chairs, and a coal-black stove in the corner, with a pot of soup beans cooking on top. Baskets filled with potatoes and dried roots and all manner of things hung from the walls.

"You'uns sit over to the bed and tell me something about yourselves. Even with Oza scarin' up folks, I don't get as many visitors as I'd wish to. It's a joy to me especially to see young'uns. I had me twelve babies, but they've scattered into the world like the tribes of Israel."

When Aunt Jennie heard that Tom was from Baltimore, Maryland, she got all excited. "I knowed me a woman once from the place called Chesapeake Bay!" she exclaimed. "You ever heard of it?"

"We stay there for a month every summer," Tom told her. "My grandfather has a house there."

Aunt Jennie nodded. "Oh, I heard it's a fine place to be. This lady I knowed, she was what you call a missionary woman. Rode up on a roan mare to preach the gospel to us, then come to learn we'd already been saved! But she was a sociable thing, and we talked and talked the whole week she was here. Got a letter from her once a month after that, all the way until her death back in 1892. She come up here in—well, let's see. I expect it was after the war—1867 or thereabouts. Mary Louise Murdock was her name."

She looked at Tom. "I don't reckon you know any of her kin."

"I don't," Tom said, sounding sorry about it. "But when we go in August, I'll see if I can find anyone related to her."

"Well, 'fore you leave here today, I'll write

down where you can send me a letter, and then you can write me and tell me if you find any of 'em. I sure would like to know. She got married late and had one baby before her change of life come. Boy named of Woodrow."

Then Aunt Jennie went about making us dinner. She peeled up five Irish potatoes, sliced them, and set them to frying in the skillet, and she got out cornmeal and mixed it with buttermilk, and poured that into another skillet to make the cornbread.

"Only animal I keep anymore is my old cow, Silvie," she told us. "Wish I had me a pig, but the last one I had run away and I didn't have the breath to go after it. Name of Joseph. Oh, I could eat about every part of a pig excepting the ears. I've heard of some who even fry up the ears, but I couldn't abide that, could you?"

Tom and I shook our heads and said no, ma'am. Aunt Jennie stirred the soup beans and cut an onion into the potatoes. "Now, every other part of the pig tastes good to me, even the feet, though Lord, it takes a year and a day

162

to get them pigs' feet clean. I like the souse you get from the head, don't you? But the last time I had a pig's head, why, I lacked the strength to cut out the eyes. Now, some eat the eyes, but I have never been favorable toward that."

I looked at Tom, who was turning green around the edges, and I thought it best to change the direction of the conversation. "My mama makes head cheese," I told Aunt Jennie. "But I was never sure if'n that was the same as souse."

"Pert' near the same," Aunt Jennie said, pulling a jar off the shelf above the stove. "Souse is when you make head cheese and then add some vinegar to it, sort of like to pickle it. Now this here is sausage that my friend Nellie Oakes brung me last time she was to the house. She cans a right plenty every fall when they butcher their hogs."

I glanced at Tom, who still didn't look quite settled. "Do you have head cheese and such in Baltimore?" I asked, trying to reel him back into the conversation.

"We have the sort of cheese you make out of milk," he replied in a shaky voice. "But I don't think that's what you're talking about."

"You just tell your mommy to get aholt of a hog's head, and I'll write down a receipt for the cooking and send it your way," Aunt Jennie promised him. "I like to mail me a letter. Don't happen but once or twice a year anymore. Might surprise you to know that I can read and write, but I most surely can. My daddy believed in it. Taught all us young'uns, boy and girl alike. You children remember the first time you looked at a word on a piece a paper and all the sudden the meaning of it just popped into your head?"

Tom said yes and told the story of when he was lying in bed recovering from getting his leg broke in five pieces from falling off a horse. His mama had left him with a stack of books two foot high, so he could look at the pictures inside to keep himself amused. One day he was flipping through a book and the word "stop" jumped out at him like a rabbit hopping off the page. "It was like I'd been struck by lightning," he declared to us. "I was five years old, and from that moment on, I read every book I could get my hands on."

"Now, breaking your leg that way, is that how come you favor your right leg so?" Aunt Jennie asked, and Tom give her a straightforward nod like it didn't bother him a bit to be asked.

"I figured it had to be something like that," Aunt Jennie said as she poked the cornbread with her finger to see if it were done. "I twisted my ankle real bad once when I was a little one. I'd just seen my first Indian out in the woods and was running home so fast I about out-paced the wind. I didn't see that root sticking up out of the ground, and Lord-a-mercy, didn't I go flying."

Tom's eyes grew big and round. "There were Indians here?" he asked, leaning across the table toward Aunt Jennie. We was eating our dinner by then, me and Tom, Aunt Jennie hovering over us and putting more food on our plates every time there was an empty spot.

"When I was a girl, there was Indians every-where. Cherokee, don't you know. President Jackson sent most of 'em off before I was full grown. He claimed this land was the white man's land, and my mommy agreed with him, but Daddy did not. Weren't many white folks in these parts then. We was one of the first families to settle. You see, my mommy and daddy had been indentured servants. You know what that is?"

Tom nodded, but I shook my head. "Well, it's like this," Aunt Jennie explained. "Some folks got to this country by signing on to be a servant to a rich family. They'd pay for you to come across the ocean from England on a ship, and you agreed to do work for 'em for how-ever many years. Daddy and Mommy come over on the same boat, and both of 'em had to work five years before they earned out their freedom. They was up in Massachusetts, where Mommy always said it were so awful cold. The minute they got the papers declaring they was free, they hitched up a mule to the wagon and come here. Mommy said this land was unsettled as unsettled could be. Nothing but Indians and deer and squirrels. They built this homestead right where you'uns are sitting, though most of it's gone now, fallen to the weather. I moved back here after my Clayton died and all my young'uns gone off into the world. A lot of this land used to be cleared, and Daddy and Mommy farmed it. Mommy birthed fourteen young'uns and raised eight of 'em."

"And were there Indians?" Tom asked, lifting up his plate so Aunt Jennie could drop another ladleful of soup beans on it. "Did you know any?"

"Like I said, they was here when I was a young'un. We didn't mix and mingle much. One winter, though, when it was so cold and the animals had gone deep into the woods, our whole family almost starved to death, except for the Indians would lay bundles of food outside that very door there. Dried jerky meat and clay pots filled with stew. I reckon that food's all what kept us alive. Daddy said they could have just as easy starved us out. But I think they knowed he tried hard to be a good neighbor. He knowed where their sacred places on the river was and never tread on 'em."

Well, we could have stayed the whole day visiting and hearing Aunt Jennie's stories, but it become clear to us after dinner that Aunt Jennie had grown weary. "I do like to take a nap of an afternoon," she admitted when we said we thought we best go. "But I hope you children will come back. You've brung up all sorts of memories to me. I'll think on 'em and see if I can't find some more Indian stories to tell you, Master Tom. And I'll write down that souse receipt for your mommy to make."

We said our good-byes and promised to come back on Tuesday morning and bring Aunt Jennie some greens from the garden and some fatback, which she'd been lacking since the loss of Joseph.

"You reckon your mama's going to make you some souse when you get back to Baltimore?" I asked Tom as we began our walk back through the woods toward home.

He laughed. "Mother doesn't step foot in the kitchen, and Sally Ann is the least adventure-some cook you've ever met in your life. Mostly she just boils things until they're hardly recognizable as food. Father complains, but Mother stays loyal to Sally Ann because she cooked for Mother's family growing up."

"I never heard of somebody having a cook come in from outside the home to make your meals, except in books. I don't know if Mama would like that or not. She's particular about her cooking."

"Look at it this way. Having a cook frees up Mother to do other things with her time, such as start schools for fishermen and take trips up to the mountains."

"I'm glad she has a cook then," I said. "Otherwise you wouldn't be here."

Tom grinned. "I'm glad about it too. Now let's keep our eyes open in case Oza appears."

I'm sorry to report that we did not see Oza on our walk down the mountain to home. But maybe we will when we come back with the creasy greens and the fatback. Maybe this time she won't disappear so fast on us and we can get to know her.

I know you must believe me addled to think such things, but if you were here with me, I feel assured you would be thinking them too.

Signed,
Your Cousin,
Arie Mae Sparks

Dear Cousin Caroline,

I just finished my chores and decided to sit down and write you before Mama puts supper on the table. The whole time I was weeding in the garden, I was pondering once again why you ain't ever wrote me back. I have written you fourteen letters in a month's time, which is a righteous good number for you to not have answered nary a one, even if your mama is against the idea of it.

Here's something I ain't told you. I have copied over every letter I've wrote you so I will remember all the things I've said. That's right, I have copied fourteen letters word for word! And every time I sit down to write a new one, I read the one I wrote before, so I won't repeat a thing. I have worked hard to make my letters interesting to you and worth the time it takes to read them.

I got to thinking out there while I was pulling up the sow thistle and the bindweed, wondering if maybe my letters never got to your house. Why, maybe Miss Ellie stole each and every one of them, so she would have gossip to share out every morning when folks come in to pick up their mail. Or maybe it's the person who's in charge of getting the mail delivered down in Raleigh. Maybe your post office man is so lazy he throws my letters away so he won't have to carry them to your house.

And then it come to me. Maybe your mama is not showing you the letters I send! Maybe every time one of my letters arrives at your door, she scoops it up and throws it in the fire! The more I thought about it, the more

I become convinced that your mama is getting in the way of you and me being friends.

I don't rightly know much about your mama, Cousin Caroline, but I remember every detail Mama ever told me. I think I remember it so well because of the way Mama's eyes would light up when she got to talking, and how dark they was by the end of the tale.

I know your mama's name is Anna and that she is two years younger than Mama, and in the year of 1908 she run off with a young doctor from Raleigh, who four years later would become your daddy. Mama says he was doing missionary work with folks from his church, tending to the sick and the dying, and your mama, Anna, went to see him because her eyes had been bothering her. "Anna always had bad allergies come summer," Mama would say. "Mommy give her all sorts of teas and tinctures, but not a one helped."

When Anna went to the doctor, he give her some drops that cleared her allergies right up, and then they fell in love. No one was surprised, as Anna Blevins was knowed to be the prettiest girl in Cranberry.

I know that your mama wrote a few letters home and then fell silent. Her daddy, our granddaddy, Elvin Blevins, rode a horse to Raleigh and found her, and she said she loved him and all her family, but she weren't ever coming back to the mountains. Once Grand-daddy and Granny Blevins died, she stopped sending word back to Stone Gap. Anna was done with us for good.

I wonder why that is. Ever since our visit with Aunt Jennie Odom, I have been feeling better about being a mountain girl. I would like to see Ruth Wells living by herself in a cabin, cooking up a pig's head and making do without help from anybody else! If I was in a war, I would want Aunt Jennie on my side, and if I was taking a long journey, I would pick her to go with me. I reckon she has enough stories to fill a hundred miles of walking.

Aunt Anna, if you are reading this letter,

please know we are fine people here, made of strong stock, and we would be proud to know you again. Well, I never knowed you in the first place, but I would like to have a chance to. Raleigh must be a fine and fancy town, but it cannot possibly compare to how pretty the mountains is in spring or how the leaves of the trees here turn yellow and red in the autumn. Folks is generous to a fault, and we have so many new things, many of which I've told of in my letters.

Please do not throw this letter in the fire, Aunt Anna! Please know my mama, Idy Blevins Sparks, pines to see your face once more and sit on the porch, talking and a-singing. She has not said this to me, but I believe it to be true. I hope you will remember that you are always welcome here, as are your doctor husband and my dear cousin Caroline, who I hope to hear from soon.

Signed,
Arie Mae Sparks

16

Dear Cousin Caroline,

When Tom come up to the house this morning, guess who he brung with him? Miss Pittman! I was waiting on the porch with a jar full of salt pork and a pillowcase filled with greens to take to Aunt Jennie, and I nearly dropped them both when I saw Miss Pittman walking up our path. I have not given her the time of day ever since I heard about what she wrote in her letter, and I still weren't interested in being friends with her.

"Look who I met on the road!" Tom called. "Miss Pittman was out for a walk, and when

I told her where we were going, she asked to come along."

Miss Pittman waved. "I hope that suits you, Arie Mae! I've never met Aunt Jennie Odom, but I've heard so many interesting stories about her!"

Well, it didn't suit me one bit, but what was I to say? I just nodded my head and joined them in the yard. Close up, Tom's cheeks looked flushed, like he was already finding the day too warm for his liking.

"Whatever do you have in that jar?" Miss Pittman asked, and I had to bite my tongue not to declare, Why, it's just the sort of food ignorant folks eat, Miss Pittman.

Instead, I held the jar up so she could see it better and said, "It's salted pork. Aunt Jennie says she lacks fatback now that her pig run off. Salted pork's just fatback that's been preserved."

"You know, I'd like to learn more about food preservation," Miss Pittman said as we headed into the woods. "I know how to can food, of course, but I know less about salting and drying it. I'd like to learn how to dry apples, for instance. Why, after our picnic the other day, Miss Keller found an apple cake that one of our mountain children had brought, and it was the most delicious thing I'd ever tasted!"

Then she give me a funny look, like she knowed the whole story behind that cake, knowed it was mine, and knowed why I hid it.

"It's easy to dry apples," I told her. "Mama can show you how in the fall. You dry 'em in the sun, but you got to watch over them so the birds don't get 'em."

"Excellent! Oh, I have so much to learn from the people here! Every day it's something new."

Now, Cousin Caroline, that surprised me. How could she be saying such a thing when she'd been writing letters off the mountain saying how ignorant and filthy we was? Why would she think she had something to learn from backwards folk such as us?

"I've been wondering something," Tom said, his breath coming out huffy and puffy, even though

we'd just started our hike. "Why do you
Aunt Jennie 'Aunt' if she's not your aunt at

I had to think on this a minute. It's fun
how you will do something your whole li
and never stop to ponder why it's so. "I gues,
when somebody gets old enough, they don't
just belong to their own people anymore, they
belong to everybody. They know all the stories
of a place, and it makes them feel like they're
kin to you. If you go talk to Uncle Cecil
Buchannan, why, he'll tell you every baby
that's been born in these mountains for the last
eighty years."

"He's a repository of memories!" Miss
Pittman proclaimed.

I nodded. "Something like that, I reckon."

We walked for a while without talking, just
enjoying the coolness of the woods on such a
warm morning and the pretty songs of the
birds. It come to me that I was feeling a bit low,
and I wondered if that was due to Miss Pittman
being there, getting in the way of me and Tom
having one of our good conversations.

And then I wondered if it was because I missed having Miss Pittman for a friend.

I almost blurted out, *Why'd you say that about us, Miss Pittman?* I so badly wanted to understand. But it was like there was a hand on my throat, squeezing on it to keep the words inside me. Then Tom started to cough. I turned to see him working to catch his breath, his face a ghosty white.

"You ought not to be making this trip, Tom Wells!" I exclaimed. "Why, look at you! You're about to collapse."

"No, I'm not," Tom insisted when he got to breathing right again. "I had a bug in my throat, that's all."

"Tom, you look pale," Miss Pittman said. "Do you think you should be making such an arduous journey?"

Tom dug into the pocket of his britches and pulled out his little book. "We're leaving for Baltimore in ten days, and I want to write down more of Aunt Jennie's stories while there's still time. Also, I need to give Aunt

Jennie my address. She has a recipe she wants to send Mother."

Well, I about fell out laughing. "You really think your mama is going to make head cheese?"

Tom cracked a grin. "No, but I'd like to see the expression on her face as she reads the list of ingredients. We better get moving, though. Mother said I have to be back by two for the wood-carving demonstration."

I got serious then. "Tom, you can't climb all the way up to Aunt Jennie's, looking all pale and ghosty the way you do. It's too much for you."

"It wasn't too much for me before, why should it be too much for me today?"

Well, what was I to do? Tom was in charge of his own self. I weren't his mama, just his friend. "At least let's go slower," I told him. "We'll get there with plenty of time for you to get your stories."

Aunt Jennie met us at the door when we got there, a welcoming smile on her face. "You'uns come back, just like you said! Oh, I have had many folks a-promise, but it's an awful long ways from anywhere up to here. I don't blame 'em for deciding against it, but it does my heart good to see you children."

"And Miss Pittman," I said. "She's come with us. She's one of them songcatchers you might have heard about."

Miss Pittman stepped forward and stuck out her hand. "I'm Betsy Pittman from the Mountain Settlement School."

Aunt Jennie looked at Miss Pittman's hand like it was some foreign species she'd never seen before. But after a moment, she reached out and took it in both of her hands, saying, "I've heard tell of your school. I reckon you're learning as much as you're teaching."

At first, Miss Pittman looked taken aback, like she was wondering why this dried apple doll of an old woman felt she could make such a declaration. But then a smile broke out over her face and she nodded her head vigorously. "Oh, yes indeed! I can't even begin to make a list of all the things I've learned, from the names of the local flora and fauna to the best way to dress a chicken. Every day adds to my education."

Aunt Jennie looked over at Tom. "You're pale, son. Let's get you inside and I'll fix you up some comfrey tea mixed with a few drops of hawthorn. It'll get your blood flowing."

We all followed Aunt Jennie into the cabin. Tom and me sat on the bed and Miss Pittman took a seat at the table. Aunt Jennie pulled some jars from that shelf over the stove and in a few minutes had the tea ready for Tom to drink. She come over to the bed with a steaming mug. "Now you drink this slow and steady, Master Tom. I hope you can bear the taste, for it's a touch bitter."

I helped Tom sit, and he took a sip of tea, making a funny face as soon as he did. "It's sour as lemons!"

"You go on and drink it anyway. I can't let you go back down that mountain till you do. In the meantime, I'll tell you a story to make it go down easier."

Tom handed me the mug to hold and pulled

his little book and a pencil from his pocket. "Arie Mae, can you write this down?"

We traded mug for book. "I'll do my best," I told him. Then I turned to Aunt Jennie and said, "Don't tell it too fast."

Aunt Jennie took a seat at the table and turned her chair so she was facing Tom directly. "Well, Master Tom, I can tell you like stories about Indians roaming these mountains, so I got to thinking about it, trying to come up with a good one for you. Then the story of little Addie Birch come to me, and that's the one I'll tell.

"By the time we children was growing up, there was more and more white folks settling in these parts, and most of 'em come here for the same reason that Mommy and Daddy had, to make a new life for themselves. But not all of 'em was like Daddy when it come to the Indians. They weren't respectful the way he was, staying away from their sacred places and only hunting what he needed.

"Well, of course, that caused many an ill

feeling on the part of the Indians, and they grew less and less friendly. Then one day we got word that a little white girl had been seen at the river with a clutch of Indian squaws doing their wash. The little girl had been dressed like an Indian, but was surely not one, her skin being white and her hair having a curl to it. All us children were so excited by this story, as we couldn't think of nothing more terrible nor more wonderful as being stolen away by Indians.

"Not long after, a neighbor man by the name of George Otis stopped by and said the white girl was believed to be Addie Birch, a child taken from over in Georgia when she was but four years old. She was ten now, and her folks had been searching for her all the time she'd been gone. So now all the white folks in these parts were putting together a party of men to capture little Addie Birch back and return her home.

"Oh, folks was in such a state! Mommy was afeared that if those men grabbed Addie away from the Indians they would come and massacre all of us in our beds. But at the same time she grieved for little Addie Birch living with them heathens and practically a wild animal by now.

"Daddy, as always, kept a calm head. He told the others that they couldn't just go and steal Addie Birch away. They would have to trade for her. Because he had always been friendly with the Indians, he said he would be the one to go and make the trade, only they needed something good as gold to trade with. But these were folks who didn't have much. Would the Indians trade Addie Birch for a bag of sugar or a yard of fabric? That didn't seem too likely.

"But then a young man name of Will Seaton come up to the house and said, 'Mr. Faught'—for that was my daddy's name, John Faught—'I have a horse that is the finest animal I have ever knowed, only she is too high-strung for plowing and of no use to me. I will trade the horse for the girl.'

"Daddy went to see the horse, and when he come back he said it was the most beautiful animal he'd ever laid eyes on, golden and tall, and any man would be proud to own her. So the next day he collected the horse and headed to the Indians' village. Me and my brothers and sisters was so excited, but Mommy, she cried and cried, fearing that the Cherokee would chop Daddy up into little pieces.

"It was hard to get anything done that day, I tell you! We was covered up with excitement! Me and my brother Samuel spent the whole day coming up with questions for to ask Addie Birch when Daddy brought her back. We was especially hoping she'd tell us all sorts of Indian secrets and words, for we was as fascinated with the Indians as young Master Tom here.

"Well, evening come and the skies grew dark, and still no Daddy. The excitement I'd been feeling all day had started to fade, and I begun to feel afraid instead. What if Mommy was right? What if Daddy was lying somewhere right that very minute, chopped all to bits?

"Somehow, we children fell asleep, even though we'd swore we would wait up till Daddy got home, even if it weren't until the next day. But one by one, we fell across the bed and our eyes fluttered closed. Then suddenly—crash!—the door flew open and it was Daddy! We all screamed when we saw him and scrambled to our feet to run and see the little captured girl, Addie Birch.

"But it turned out, she weren't there. 'Would they not accept the horse in trade, John?' Mommy asked, but Daddy shook his head.

"'No, they saw the merit of that horse, just as any man would,' he said, taking a seat at the table right here where I sit and pulling off his boots. 'It was the girl. She didn't want to leave.'

"Mommy looked as though someone had slapped her. 'How could that be? Did you even see her?'

"'Oh, I seen her all right. They brought her into the hut and showed her to me. She's a pretty little thing, and they say she's smart, but when I spoke to her, she acted like she didn't understand me. There was a woman who spoke English and Cherokee, and she told the girl what I was saying, that I'd come to trade for her and bring her back to her folks. Well, the girl started moaning and crying and shaking her head no. I thought the Indians was going to make her go with me, but finally they turned to me and said, "No trade."'

"Well, we just couldn't believe that! But Daddy said he reckoned that if she was captured when she was four, she probably didn't remember much if anything about her old life. He said it might not be a kindness to send her back, given how set she was in her ways.

"Six months later, the army come in and made the trade, this time for five Cherokee braves they'd been holding in their jail. So she did go back to her folks. But here's the interesting part of the story to me. Four more years passed, and we pretty much forgot all about Addie Birch. And then one day, Daddy was out in the field when he saw a young woman walking toward him. When she reached him, she asked if he knew where Al-Le-Teek's camp was, and Daddy said no, but he reckoned if she headed for the river she'd find someone who

189

could tell her, and then he told her how to get to the river from where they was.

"Of course, he thought it odd that a white girl would come looking for a Cherokee camp, but in them days, folks didn't meddle much, not even with young'uns. So he watched her walk off, but right as she was about to disappear over the ridge, he called out, 'Addie Birch!' Sure enough, didn't that girl turn around and look before she took off running!"

"So she come back!" I said, scribbling down the last words of the story. "She didn't want to live with white folks anymore and she walked all the way back from Georgia!"

"That's what I think," Aunt Jennie said. "Weren't too long after that the Cherokees was sent out West, and I reckon Addie Birch went with them."

Well, Cousin Caroline, I found that to be a satisfying tale, and I reckon Tom did too. When the telling was over, he looked tired, but there was a better color to his cheeks. I

190

handed him back his book, which he put on the bed beside him, patting its cover as though it contained considerable treasures.

All of us was quiet as we trekked back down the mountain to home. Tom was conserving his strength, and I was thinking on the story Aunt Jennie had told us. How I wished I had lived in the time of the Cherokee and could have knowed me one or two!

Miss Pittman seemed lost in her own thoughts as well. But when we got to the home place, she put her hand on my arm and said, "Arie Mae, thank you for taking me to meet Aunt Jennie. Every day that I live and breathe in these mountains, I find it more and more satisfying to call them home."

I stared at her. "You think of this place as your home? Even with the way it is? I mean, with some folks being ignorant and all?"

I couldn't bring myself to say "ignorant and filthy," even if I knowed that's what Miss Pittman thought about us.

Miss Pittman gave me a long look.

"Whatever would cause you to say that, child?"

"Didn't—well, didn't you write that letter?" I asked, my face hot in the sun. "That's what folks are saying."

"That confounded letter!" Miss Pittman said, her voice shaking. "I rue the day I wrote it. I understand why people are angry with me, but what no one understands is that I meant well. I truly did! When we first arrived, we met people who didn't take baths all winter. We saw babies with open sores on their skin and children with lice crawling through their hair. It was shocking and terrible."

"But it weren't a true picture of this place," I told her, surprised that the words I'd been longing to say finally freed themselves from my throat. I was almost whispering when I said, "It weren't the least bit true of all kinds of folks who live up here."

Tom come over and stood by my side. "I don't think it's true either, Miss Pittman."

Miss Pittman took in a deep breath. "Yes, I know that now. We've met so many wonderful people since then. Hardworking people who just needed a helping hand to make their lot in life a little easier. That's why we decided to start our school, don't you see? We did it out of love, Arie Mae. I hope you believe me when I tell you that."

All I could do was nod. And here it is, late in the evening, and Cousin Caroline, I am still studying the meaning of Miss Pittman's words. I have thought about what Mama says, that people run good and bad, and no one is made up of all one and none of the other. I know Miss Pittman has a lot of good in her, and I reckon she's telling the truth when she says she feels this place is now her home. I believe her when she says she and Miss Keller started their school out of love for the poor people living here.

It just makes me wonder if love is the be-all and end-all that everybody thinks it is.

Signed,
Your Cousin,
Arie Mae Sparks

Dear Cousin Caroline,

Today my heart is breaking. Outside the
sun shines like everything is just the same,
and I wish I could yank it out of the sky.

Last night, as I walked down to the settlement school to listen to Mama sing, I felt as
though the world was mine wrapped in a bow.
There we was, all us Sparks as fancy as we
knowed how to get, with Mama so cheerful
because she was going to sing in front of folks,
and Daddy acting jolly because he loved to
play his fiddle for a crowd. Us children was
as excited as could be, even Baby John, who

wriggled his toes and giggled up a storm all the way down the mountain.

If I had one worry nipping at the back of my mind, it was whether or not Miss Pittman and Miss Keller would keep up their end of the bargain. Mama was singing at their school. Would they come to the barn dance next week? Whichever way, if they did or if they didn't come next Saturday, I would know whether me and Miss Pittman could ever again be friends.

But even that worry could not cut into my good feelings about the evening. The singing was to take place on the first floor of the main school building with a big crowd in attendance. When we got there, the room was filled up with Baltimore folks. I recognized the children, but many of the adults was new to me. There was seven in all, four women and three men, and they nodded and smiled when they seen us, like our whole family was the star attraction. They looked like a friendly enough bunch. I wondered if they would be sad to leave us next week, or if they was so excited to start their own school that they couldn't wait to go.

And for the first time, I wondered about them fishermen who was about to get themselves a school. Did they even want one? That is the question that school starters don't ever seem to ask.

Me and James and Lucille and Harlan planned to sit with Tom and Ruth and the others. I of course was going to sit smack-dab next to Tom so I could look at his book with the stories he'd been collecting. I'd not seen him since our last visit to Aunt Jennie's, and I wanted to read again the story of Addie Birch so that I'd remember it all my days.

"There's Ruth over thataway," Harlan said, pointing to a table where a punch bowl and cups was laid out. We started walking in her direction, but as soon as she seen us, she lickety-split run from the room.

James looked at me with eyebrows raised. "What d'you reckon is wrong with her?"

"Maybe she's heartbroke about having to bid me farewell come next week," Harlan said. "I think she's sweet on me."

Lucille leaned over and popped him in the arm. "I don't know what's come over you these past few weeks, Harlan Boyd, but I'm about to set you to rights."

Harlan looked Lucille straight in the eye for almost three whole seconds before he lowered his head and shoved his hands in his pockets. "Ah, I'm just having some fun, Lucille. Ain't a feller allowed to have some fun ever' once in a while?"

Well, me and James was laughing and shaking our heads when out of nowhere Ruth Wells stood smack right in front of us, pointing a bony finger in my face.

"You're the most selfish girl I've ever met, Arie Mae Sparks! Mother told you Tom was ill and shouldn't go off climbing mountains, but did you listen? Not for a minute!"

I took a step back. At the same time, James took a step closer to me and grabbed aholt of my arm to keep me steady. "I don't rightly know what you're talking about, Ruth," I replied in a shaky voice. Except that I did, of course. Hadn't Tom gone up to Aunt Jennie's two days before, even though his skin was pale and he couldn't hardly breathe? Hadn't I let him?

Ruth glared at me, her hands on her hips. "Tom's gone home, where the doctors say he'll have to stay in bed for the next month if he's to recover. Father came and retrieved him this morning."

If James hadn't been holding on to me, I reckon I would have fallen to the floor. "Me and Miss Pittman tried to stop him," I told her. "But he wouldn't be stopped."

"Miss Pittman is the one who told us of your ill-advised trip," Ruth informed me. "She feels terribly guilty about it, but of course she didn't know about Tom's heart condition."

"He told me it weren't as bad as your mama made it sound."

Ruth pursed her lips. "And you believed him. How ignorant can you be?"

That's when the tears come to my eyes, because I knowed she was right. I was ignorant. I'd not paid attention to the true facts of the situation. Anybody would have knowed that Tom shouldn't have been climbing up to Aunt Jennie's. Why, the second trip up he could hardly breathe. How could I have believed him when he'd said he was coughing because he'd swallowed a bug? A bug! That right there just went to show how ignorant I was.

James said, "Come on, Arie Mae, let's go sit down," but I wouldn't budge. I was going to stand there and let Ruth Wells yell at me as much as she wanted. She had a right to.

And then, to my surprise, Lucille piped up. "Now wait one minute, Ruth Wells! Arie Mae is not your brother's keeper! If he chased her up the mountain, well, that's not her fault, now is it? I'm sorry that he's ailing, but I reckon if you were to ask him would he do it again, he'd say yes."

I tell you, Ruth's mouth dropped open into a big, wide O, and oh, didn't she give Lucille the most icy stare?

I stared, too. I stared like Lucille had took aholt of my shoulders and shook me. It was just the way she said. Everything Tom did, he did it because he wanted to. I thought about him at the creek, hardly budging in the face of that bear. He might have had a bad leg and a weak heart, but that didn't stop him from living his life full to the hilt.

Maybe I weren't ignorant. Maybe sometimes Tom Wells was a reckless fool.

But he was still my own true friend.

Ruth stuck her nose in the air, as if Lucille weren't worth listening to. Then she turned to me and said, "Tom said to tell you he lost his book, and he needs you to find it. He said you'd know what that means."

Then she turned on her heel and walked out of the room. James watched her go and then said, "She always did have something up her craw. I guess it's 'cause nobody likes her all that much."

"Oh, I like her," Lucille said, brushing a spot of dust from her sleeve. "I just don't think it's right for her to blame Arie Mae for Tom's troubles. It's not her fault he had to go home."

And that's when it truly hit me. Tom had gone home. Who was I going to have adventures with if Tom weren't here? Who would help me collect interesting stories?

"Come on, Arie Mae," Harlan said, grabbing my hand. "Let's go get us a seat in the front row so we can hear Mama real good."

So all of us children went to the very front of the room and sat right in front of where Mama would sing and Daddy would fiddle. I had James to my left and Harlan to my right, and as soon as we sat down, Mama came over and put Baby John on my lap. I hugged him to me tight, hoping that the nearness of him would keep my heart from breaking half in two.

Mama and Daddy come to the front of the stage, and Mama looked so beautiful, even if her dress was homemade and not from Mrs. Green on Eager Street in Baltimore. She sang all the songs we love so well, such as "Barbry

Allen" and "Fair Rosamond," and Daddy played fiddle behind her. All us children snuggled in together, letting the music wash over us, feeling our pride at first, but then just feeling like our own selves. We knowed we was rich, Cousin Caroline, even if we was poor.

And still, my heart is broke, and I fear it will never mend.

Signed,
Your Cousin,
Arie Mae Sparks

Dear Cousin Caroline,

I woke this morning with only one thought on my mind, and that was to fetch Tom's book. I snuck out of bed as not to wake Lucille or Baby John, and I went to find James, who was, as I expected, still asleep in the room he shares with Harlan. I poked him in the side a couple of times and whispered "Shh!" when his eyes popped wide open.

"If you'll do my chores this morning, I'll do yourn this afternoon," I whispered. "And if Mama asks where I am, tell her I went sassafras hunting."

"Is that what you're really doing?" James mumbled in a sleepy voice.

"I'll pick some to make it true."

James rolled back over with a snort. "All right then."

The morning dew soaked my feet as I crossed the yard to the woods. I knowed the first place to look for Tom's book was Aunt Jennie's. I remember handing it to him when we was last at her place, and him setting it on the bed beside him. He must have never slipped it back into his pocket, but left it lying there. Aunt Jennie would have put it in a safe place, I reckoned, and it would be waiting for me when I knocked on her door.

I ran fast as a jackrabbit up the woody path toward Pilgrim's Gap. I wanted to fetch Tom's book and give it to Ruth that very day. It would make him feel better if he could look at all the stories he wrote down while he was in these mountains, I just knowed it. Oh, I wished he could have been there to hear Mama sing the night before! He would have filled many a page with those old songs of hers, full of murder and love and shallow graves.

As I got close to Miss Sary's, I thought about stopping in to say hello, but I feared disturbing Pastor Campbell as he wrote his Sunday sermon, which according to Miss Sary he liked to work on first thing of a morning. According to Miss Sary, sometimes Pastor Campbell walked about outdoors with paper and pen in hand, hoping that nature would inspire godly words in him.

When I heard a rustling off the path, I figured that it must be Pastor Campbell out walking and writing. But then something caught my eye, something shining like a coin held up to the light.

It was a girl. It was a shining girl. She wore a white dress that was so crisp and clean, it must have been made brand-new that morning. She smiled when she saw me and said, "I'm lost. Could you help me find my way home?"

I stood perfectly still. "Oza?"

"You know me?" the girl asked, and her smile got even bigger. "Do you know my mama? Her name is Jennie Odom, and she lives over to Pilgrim's Gap."

"I know her," I replied in a shaky voice. "I'm heading that way now."

"Can you show me how to get there?"

Every part of me was a-trembling, but I said, "I'll show you the way, Oza."

Only it was her who trotted up the path ahead of me! I had to hurry my steps to keep up with her, and a few times she dropped away from sight and I was sure that I'd lost her. But then there she was again, waiting for me to catch up, still smiling.

We reached the place where you could see smoke rising out of Aunt Jennie's cabin. "Your mama lives just over that ridge," I told Oza. "We'll be there shortly."

"Thank you, Arie Mae," she said. And then, just like that, she disappeared.

My heart was thumping so hard in my chest, I thought it was going to bust through. Oh my goodness! My legs shook, and every part of me went cold and then hot.

"Oza!" I called. "Oza, where are you?"

Nobody answered. I looked all around me, but she was gone. I was alone in a clearing, the only sound around me the chatter of squirrels and a lone bird chirping. Had I really seen the ghost of Oza Odom? Or was my mind all twisted and turned from the heartbreak of losing my own true friend, Tom Wells?

When I saw the tree stump in the middle of the clearing, I thought to sit and catch my breath and calm my mind before traveling on to Aunt Jennie's. But when I reached the stump, I noticed something laying smack-dab at its center.

It was Tom's book. Oza had led me straight to it.

Oh, didn't I grab it and hold it tight! It was like having a piece of Tom right there with me. But what was it doing out here? I examined the pages and saw they was wet around the edges, as though the book had been lying on the grass and had soaked up a bit of morning dew.

"Oza?" I called out again, and a voice called back, "Arie Mae?"

Only it weren't Oza's voice, but Aunt Jennie's.

She come into the clearing, stooped over and walking with a stick. "Tom left that book at my place when you'uns were there last," she said when she saw me. "I thought I'd walk it down to Miss Sary's yesterday afternoon so she could give it to him, and then I got curious and sat down right on that stump to read it. I reckon I left it there. Don't look any worse for the wear, now do it?"

I shook my head. "No, ma'am. Just a little wet here and there."

"You see Oza this morning?"

"Yes, ma'am. Well, I seen somebody—or something."

Aunt Jennie lowered herself slow and careful as could be until she was sitting down on the stump. "Oh, it were Oza all right. I seen her run past the window."

I sat next to her. "Don't it spook you to see her?"

"Arie Mae, I'm a hundred years old. Nothing spooks me. I just wish she'd go on over to the other side, to be with her daddy. I've asked her to, but she seems to like it here."

I held up Tom's book and looked at it. "Tom got sick and had to go home to Baltimore. I reckon it's halfway my fault. I knowed his heart weren't good enough to come up here. Only he told me it was. He were stubborn when it come to doing what he wanted."

"Everybody tells a lie from time to time. Tom's just the same. Weren't your fault he come up here, Arie Mae. He did what he wanted to do. Now what you aim to do with that book?"

"Give it to his sister, for her to take to him." I flipped through a few of the pages, reading a line here and there. "Though Lord knows if she'll give it back to him. It's filled with ghost stories, and she's against them. Maybe it's best to mail it."

"His address is in there too," Aunt Jennie said. "I saw it on the inside cover. It's 1306 St. Paul Street. Why, you could just mail that book to him. Everybody likes to get something in the mail."

That's when I knowed exactly what to do. "I

wish I had a pencil. Tom always had a pencil with him to write things down right away so he wouldn't forget, and I don't want to forget what I want to tell."

Well, I wouldn't have believed it if I hadn't seen it with my own eyes, but didn't Aunt Jennie pluck Tom's pencil from behind her ear and hand it to me! Then she used her walking stick to push herself back up, saying, "I reckon I'll leave you to it. You come visit me now. Bring me some more greens!"

"I'll come tomorrow," I promised, opening Tom's book and finding the first blank page. There I wrote the story of Oza the ghost, and when I was done I cried a little, wishing so bad that Tom had seen her this morning too.

Signed,
Your Cousin,
Arie Mae Sparks

19

Dear Cousin Caroline,

I don't believe I could dance another step in my life, not even if you paid me good money. Last night we danced till our toes was about to fall off. Us children got silly after a while, not so much dancing as running around the barn, just a-singing and a-yelling, chasing one another in a game of Crack the Whip. Usually the grown-ups will call for us to settle down when we get that way, but there was too much good cheer for bossing children around last night. We was allowed to be as high-spirited as we wished to.

211

Folks begin to gather at the barn around seven o'clock so they'd be ready for when the National Barn Dance radio show with your host George D. Hay started up at eight. It seemed like everybody in the world was there last night, even old Uncle Cecil Buchannan, who had come with some of his mostly grown grandbabies.

At eight o'clock, Daddy turned on the radio, and George D. Hay's voice come out saying, "Welcome, welcome, welcome! We're here in the old hayloft in Chicago, Illinois, for another Saturday night at the National Barn Dance!" Everybody whooped and hollered at that, especially us children. Then the sound of fiddles started up, and Uncle Cecil Buchannan got us dancing in a Virginia reel, calling out the steps. "Head lady and foot gentleman forward and back!" he shouted, and then, "Forward again with both hands round!"

Oh, we clapped and sung and stomped. But if I had my ears bent toward Uncle Cecil, I had my eyes glued to the door. Would Miss

Keller and Miss Pittman come like Mama had asked them to? I wondered what Daddy would do if they didn't. He'd been feeling more kindly toward them after playing fiddle at the school for the Baltimore folks last Friday, and it would be a shame to see his goodwill go to waste.

Mama says a watched pot never boils, and I guess she must be right, for it was when I finally unstuck my eyes from the door and went to get a sip of lemonade that Miss Keller and Miss Pittman made their entrance. The reaction to them being there was mixed, as most everyone had heard from Thelma Maycomb and her mama about Miss Pittman's letter. Many leaned toward forgiveness, as the letter had been written some time ago and they felt the songcatchers' school had brought a gracious plenty to us. So there were greetings and hellos as they come in and looked for where to stand and who to speak with, but some whispers and icy looks, too.

Daddy himself went over to say hello, which I thought was neighborly of him. He had heard about Miss Pittman's letter, but he was inclined to not judge too harshly. "I reckon she might have felt taken aback when she come to our mountains, especially if it were to a rough bunch such as the Nidiffers and the Fowlkeses she first went to visit," Daddy had said when James shared Will Maycomb's report. "And she might be right that we don't meet up to the world's standards. But as long as we meet up to our standards, then what's that to worry us?"

I was wondering if Miss Keller and Miss Pittman would join in the dancing. There was two types of dancing going on, the square dance in the middle of the room and the clog dancing on the edges. Some folks wore taps on their shoes that made it sound like tiny pistols was going off every time their toes hit the floor. I think both kinds of dancing are fine, and it depends on my mood as to which one I favor. Sometimes stomping your feet and jumping around is mighty satisfying, but other times I like to swing around with a partner, even if it's just Harlan Boyd.

The radio show dancing went on for an hour, but neither Miss Keller nor Miss Pittman had tapped a single toe. With each step I took, I stomped a little harder, wishing I had the nerve to tell them a thing or two about being snooty and stuck-up and too big for their own britches. They might as well have not come at all if they wasn't going to join the party!

Oh, I was a-fuming and a-fussing in my own mind, and a few times I stomped on Harlan's toes and he yelped like a dog. "Ease on back, Arie Mae!" he'd cry. "We ain't at war!"

When the National Barn Dance show was over, Daddy turned off the radio. That meant it was time for him and Mr. Peacock and anybody else who brung a fiddle or a guitar or a banjo to get tuned up. The musicians huddled in a corner, leaning their heads together, plucking their strings, until everybody was on the same note. Chatter and laughter rose around them as folks got ready for the second half of the dance. A few of the older boys slipped out, most likely to make mischief of one sort or another, and some of the young'uns piled up on bales of hay and fell fast asleep.

"We're gonna start out with 'Cluck Old Hen,'" Daddy informed the crowd once the band was tuned up. "Now, this is one of our favorites, and we hope it's one of yourn, too."

You can't help but to dance to "Cluck Old Hen," and all us children run to the center of the barn, even the younger ones who didn't know much about dancing and just liked to jump up and down. The grown-ups made a circle around us, clapping and a-stomping. "Cluck old hen! A-doodily-do," they sang. "Cluck old hen, cock-a-doodily doo!"

Us children linked hands and made a skipping circle, singing, "Cluck old hen, cluck and sing, ain't laid an egg since late last spring!"

We was going faster and faster, and then someone broke into the circle next to me. Miss Pittman! She sung the words right along with us, and when the song ended, she clapped her hands like she weren't ever going to stop.

"Oh, Arie Mae," she said, her breath coming out hard. "Your daddy has converted me to the fiddle!"

And she danced every song after that, and guess what? That hair that's always pulled back so tight on her head? It started coming loose, and Lord, it was pretty the way Miss Pittman looked like a young girl, curls all around her face.

I think getting converted to the fiddle is just what Miss Pittman needed.

This morning we set off to church, all of us feeling tired and weary from dancing. But Mama is not a person who says, "Let's lay about this Sunday morning and forget about worshipping the Lord!" So off we went, and the whole way I was thinking about Miss Pittman. I reckon she's sorry for what she wrote, don't you? I reckon she might be feeling a little ignorant herself now that she knows us as good as she does. It takes time to get to know people. You got to listen to their stories, and you got to tell your stories back. It all goes back and forth, back and forth, until one day you turn into friends.

Until that time, I expect it's best to keep your opinions to yourself.

I am still missing Tom something fierce and have written him two letters since sending him his book, telling him everything that has happened since he went off the mountain back to home. Now, Tom is somebody who likes to hear your stories and that's the truth. I am hoping that he's also the sort of person who writes back and tells a few stories of his own, unlike some other people I could name.

Signed,
Your Cousin,
Arie Mae Sparks

Dear Cousin Caroline,

I weren't expecting anything when I went to the post office this morning, but I hoped I might find a letter from Tom waiting for me. It has been ten days since I sent him his book. But, I reminded myself as I walked down the path, he is sick and might not be able to write a letter. It might be weeks and weeks until I hear a word.

Still, I was hoping. When Miss Ellie seen me walk in, she got such a big grin on her face, I thought it must be so! There must be a letter. Oh, my heart just jumped up and down, I was so happy.

"Arie Mae Sparks, looks like Santy Claus done come for you today!" she called out, and then she run around from the back of the counter, her arms filled with all manner of things!

"All that's for me?" I cried, counting two boxes and two envelopes. "How could that be?"

"Well, it ain't all for you," Miss Ellie said. "One of them letters is for your mama. It's from Raleigh. Now, don't she got kin in Raleigh?"

"My mama's sister lives in Raleigh," I said, and the little hairs on my arm stood straight up.

Miss Ellie dumped all that mail into my arms. "Well? Ain't ya gonna open it?"

I was afeared that if I even so much as looked at what I held, I'd melt into a puddle on the floor. "I reckon I'll take it home and open it there. Kind of hold on to the surprise for a little bit longer."

"Oh, you ain't no fun, Arie Mae!" Miss Ellie said with a pout. "Well, I want you to come back tomorrow and tell me what you got, you hear?"

I run all the way home, still not letting myself look at who them packages and letters was from. "Mama!" I cried as soon as I reached our yard. "Mama! You got a letter!"

Well, Mama come running out of the house, Baby John in her arms, Lucille and Harlan on her heels. "A letter? Who on earth would be sending me a letter?"

"It's from Raleigh, Mama."

Mama put her hand over her heart. "From Raleigh."

"I got a letter too, but I ain't let myself look to see who it's from yet. And two packages."

"Who's them packages from, Arie Mae?" Harlan asked, peering over my shoulder. "Anything good in 'em?"

That's when I looked and seen that one package was from T. Wells, 1306 St. Paul Street, Baltimore, Maryland! The other didn't have no return address. "One's from Tom," I reported. "And the other one's a mystery. And I got a letter, too."

221

"Let Mama read her letter first," Lucille said, taking Baby John out of Mama's arms. "Mama, you sit down on the step right here and read. You can read it out loud."

"I'm too nervous to read it out loud," Mama said, sitting down on the top step. Careful as could be, she tore open the envelope. She pulled out two sheets of paper, and as soon as she seen the handwriting, she gasped. "It's from Anna!" she cried, and then she bust out sobbing.

"Read the letter, Mama!" Harlan told her. "You can cry all you want later."

We all sat there on the steps, quiet as could be. I was dying to open my parcels and my own letter, but I thought Mama should go first.

"All right then, I'll read," Mama said, wiping her nose with her apron. "It's from my sister Anna in Raleigh," she began, and then she cried a little bit more before reading on. "She says she misses me so much and she feels terrible about not writing in ever so long." Mama paused, cried, read some more and reported, "She says

she has read every single one of Arie Mae's letters, and they have made her homesick
something awful . . . And that she hadn't
shown any of them to Caroline until the day
she wrote this letter, because up until then . . .
until then Caroline didn't know she had any
cousins in the mountains."

"She didn't even know about us?" Lucille
harrumphed. "What kind of manners is that,
not to tell your own child she has cousins?"

"Hush now, Lucille," Mama said, sniffing a
bit. "Anna says she has been in the wrong all
these years, and she wants to come visit and
see the old home place just as soon as she can,
which will probably be next month." Well, that
set Mama off to crying for a long spell, and we
all leaned over and patted her, trying to soothe
her a bit.

"Did she give my letters to Caroline then?"
I asked. "Does Caroline know I exist yet?"

Mama nodded. "Anna says Caroline's going
to write you a nice letter back. Well, you got a
letter today, didn't you? Who's it from?"

And that's when I finally let myself look at the return address. Sure, enough, it said Raleigh, North Carolina. "I think this is it," I said, my fingers all a-trembling. "I think this is the letter from Caroline."

"Read it, Arie Mae!" Harlan cried. "Let's hear about our cousin in Raleigh!"

But I couldn't bring myself to read it in front of them. I had told Caroline so much that I ain't told them, I felt our friendship to be a private thing.

"How about I open this package from Tom?" I asked, and they all cheered. So I opened up the box and what did I find, but a book just like Tom's and a note saying he was feeling much better and he was sending me a book for me to write my own stories in. "Please tell me all the ghost stories you hear, Arie Mae," he wrote, "and let me know if you see Oza again."

"Oza Odom?" Lucille asked, leaning toward me as though to read the letter herself. "You seen her?"

I folded it back up and said, "I'll tell you

about it later. Now let's see what's in this other parcel."

Turned out the other parcel was from Aunt Jennie! She'd sent me a copy of her recipe book with a note that said, "Please copy out the souse receipt and send it on to Tom Wells."

"I guess I'll go do that directly," I said, standing up and gathering my things together. I leaned over and give Mama a hug. "I'm happy Aunt Anna wrote you a letter, Mama."

Mama looked at me a long moment. "I gave up on my sister when I should have kept trying to reach her. I'm so glad you didn't give up on your cousin. It means the world to me that you two are friends."

Cousin Caroline, I could barely keep still as I sat on my bed to read your letter. I feared it would be short and polite, even though the envelope had a nice heft to it. What if you had nothing to say to me, only "Thank you for your letters, I hope you are fine." Oh, I couldn't bear it if that was the case.

But as you and me both know, that weren't the case at all.

Thank you for the picture you sent! It is such a nice one, the way your face is shining and full of life. Why, it makes me feel like we have knowed each other for years and years and have always been the best of friends.

I am sorry to say we don't share much of a resemblance, but you and Lucille have similar eyes, and that has made Lucille happy as can be. She says she is going to write you a long letter all about herself with lots of details and a lock of her hair. You don't have to write her back, but she will be your devoted servant if you do.

And thank you for telling me about what your school is like. I don't know that I'd care to go to a school that was just girls, especially when some of them sound awful mean. I think any girl named Bertha is bound to be sour, and you are wise to stay out of her way. I'm happy to hear that your teacher, Miss Gardner, is sweet-natured, and that you are her pet. I wish

Miss Sary's school had a chalkboard so I could clap erasers against the brick wall at the end of the day the way you do.

There is one part of your letter I have read over and over again, where you said my letters have set straight why your mama's apple stack cake has always been your favorite and why you have always felt homesick for a place you never been. My letters made you see that you are a mountain girl just the same as me.

Now, don't that just make perfect sense? Your mama is a mountain girl, after all. I think when you come to visit, you won't feel homesick no more because you will be right at home.

And yes, we will do all them things you asked to do once you get here. We'll hike up to Aunt Jennie's and go looking for Oza, and if you are truly wanting to learn to make souse, then I'm sure Mama will be happy to show you how, but you might think twice after you see the recipe.

And yes, we will visit Miss Sary and look at her encyclopedia with James and make plans for our travels, and we will go to a barn dance of a Saturday night and I will teach you all the words to "Cluck Old Hen."

Lucille can't wait for you to meet Chandelier and James is wondering if you are the kind of girl who likes to go fishing. I told him that I thought you most likely was.

Oh, we will have so many adventures when you come to visit! But you know what I most look forward to? Sitting on the porch of an evening, where I will tell you all of my stories and you will tell me all of yours. For now, I will put your picture beside my bed and think of you each night before I go to sleep. I am counting the days until your arrival. Until then, I remain

Your Cousin and Own True Friend,
Arie Mae Sparks

Acknowledgements

I would like to thank Caitlyn Dlouhy for once again making the magic happen, and Jessica Sit for being a fabulous magician's assistant. Thanks to Michael McCartney, who did such a marvelous job designing this book, and to Clare McGlade, whose copyedits made the book a better place to be. Thanks to Justin Chanda, world's best publisher and rooftop gardener, for his ongoing support. Thanks to Doug Broyles, for sharing his knowledge of Old Time music and trying to teach me to play the fiddle, bless his heart. Thanks to the good folks of the N.C. Folklife Institute for letting me raid their archives. A tip of the hat is owed to David Whisnant, whose book <u>All That is Native and Fine: The Politics of Culture in an American Region</u> inspired this story. Much love to Amy Graham and Danielle Paul for their constant encouragement, and to Clifton, Jack, Will and Travis Dowell for being the best family (and dog) a writer could ask for.